Her voice was the first thing he'd noticed about her back then.

The soft breathlessness of Gabby's voice had held something sweet and kind that soothed the savage creature raging inside him.

At seventeen, cool Joe Carpenter didn't have time to waste on thirteen-year-old skinny girls with kind voices, not when high school girls fell all over each other offering to give him anything he wanted.

But touching that bitter, angry place he'd closed off to the world, her voice made him remember her over the years as she grew into a woman, made him lift his head in baffled awareness whenever he heard that soft voice reminding him all the world wasn't hard and mean and nasty.

And now her voice sent his pulse into overdrive with its pure breathlessness. And to think that now, after all this time, they were going to be neighbors....

Dear Reader,

Happy Holidays! Our gift to you is all the very best Romance has to offer, starting with *A Kiss, a Kid and a Mistletoe Bride* by RITA-Award winning author Lindsay Longford. In this VIRGIN BRIDES title, when a single dad returns home at Christmas, he encounters the golden girl he'd fallen for one magical night a lifetime ago. Can his kiss—and his kid—win her heart and make her a mistletoe mom?

Rising star Susan Meier continues her TEXAS FAMILY TIES miniseries with *Guess What? We're Married!* And no one is more shocked than the amnesiac bride in this sexy, surprising story! In *The Rich Gal's Rented Groom,* the next sparkling installment of Carolyn Zane's THE BRUBAKER BRIDES, a rugged ranch hand poses as Patsy Brubaker's husband at her ten-year high school reunion. But this gal voted Most Likely To Succeed won't rest till she wins her counterfeit hubby's heart! BUNDLES OF JOY meets BACHELOR GULCH in a fairy-tale romance by beloved author Sandra Steffen. When a shy beauty is about to accept *another* man's proposal, her true-blue *true* love returns to town, bearing *Burke's Christmas Surprise.*

Who wouldn't want to be *Stranded with a Tall, Dark Stranger*— especially an embittered ex-cop in need of a good woman's love? Laura Anthony's tale of transformation is perfect for the holidays! And speaking of transformations... Hayley Gardner weaves an adorable, uplifting tale of a Grinch-like hero who becomes a Santa Claus daddy when he receives *A Baby in His Stocking.*

And in the New Year, look for our fabulous new promotion FAMILY MATTERS and Romance's first-ever six-book continuity series, LOVING THE BOSS, in which office romance leads six friends down the aisle.

Happy Holidays!

Mary-Theresa Hussey
Senior Editor, Silhouette Romance

Please address questions and book requests to:
Silhouette Reader Service
U.S.: 3010 Walden Ave., P.O. Box 1325, Buffalo, NY 14269
Canadian: P.O. Box 609, Fort Erie, Ont. L2A 5X3

VIRGIN BRIDES

A KISS, A KID AND A MISTLETOE BRIDE

LINDSAY LONGFORD

Silhouette

ROMANCE™

Published by Silhouette Books

America's Publisher of Contemporary Romance

To my very own "scullery wenches" who gave of their time and of themselves on a difficult day: Suzette Edelen, Patty Copeland, Myrna Topol and Margaret Watson. You worked like *dawgs,* you were sunshine through the clouds and you gave me the greatest gift of all: yourselves. I don't have words eloquent enough to thank you.

 SILHOUETTE BOOKS

ISBN 0-373-19336-X

A KISS, A KID AND A MISTLETOE BRIDE

Copyright © 1998 by Jimmie Morel

Printed in U.S.A.

Books by Lindsay Longford

Silhouette Romance

Jake's Child #696
Pete's Dragon #854
Annie and the Wise Men #977
The Cowboy, the Baby and the Runaway Bride #1073
The Cowboy and the Princess #1115
Undercover Daddy #1168
Daddy by Decision #1204
A Kiss, a Kid and a Mistletoe Bride #1336

Silhouette Intimate Moments

Cade Boudreau's Revenge #390
Sullivan's Miracle #526
Renegade's Redemption #769

Silhouette Shadows

Lover in the Shadows #29
Dark Moon #53

LINDSAY LONGFORD,

like most writers, is a reader. She even reads toothpaste labels in desperation! A former high school English teacher with an M.A. in literature, she began writing romances because she wanted to create stories that touched readers' emotions by transporting them to a world where good things happened to good people and happily-ever-after is possible with a little work.

Her first book, *Jake's Child,* was nominated for Best New Series Author, Best Silhouette Romance, and received a Special Achievement Award for Best First Series Book from *Romantic Times Magazine.* It was also a finalist for Romance Writers of America's RITA Award for Best First Book. Her Silhouette Romance *Annie and the Wise Men* won the RITA for the best Traditional Romance of 1993.

Dear Reader,

Recently my nineteen-year-old son casually asked, "So, Mom, were you a virgin bride?"

After I picked myself up off the floor and hemmed and hawed a few minutes, I answered him. Then we talked for two hours about love and sex and commitment. And, no, I didn't blush!

Kids. They'll surprise you every time.

I was touched by his explanation that for him, sex without emotion wasn't worth much. Love, he explained with all the wisdom of his accumulated years, is the emotional bond that makes everything meaningful because you care about the other person's feelings as much as you care about your own. And the one you love puts your feelings first, too. Love is worth waiting for, he said.

When I thought about Gabrielle, the heroine of *A Kiss, a Kid and a Mistletoe Bride,* I wanted a heroine who was virgin by choice, not because she'd never had the opportunity to date, not because she'd had a terrible childhood. I wanted a smart, caring woman who knew the value of her own heart—and body—especially in today's risky world. She knows what she wants, what she deserves, and she's not willing to settle for less. Gabrielle is a woman whose first love is her only and forever love.

First love has an incredible power. It's the one we never forget. Sometimes we're lucky and our first love is the right love, the person who completes us and makes us better for knowing him. That man becomes our time capsule, the guy who remembers us when we were young, the person who knows us at our deepest levels, both good and bad, and still loves us. My husband of thirty-three years was my first love, a boy when we fell in love, and a man of courage and kindness. I think he would be proud of his son, who knows the value of love.

First love is special, like no other, and that's what I wanted for Gabrielle. Like her, may you, too, discover love with all its magic and power, whether it's your first love, only love or last love.

Lindsay Longford

Chapter One

"**Y**ou can't have that Christmas tree. It's mine."

The voice came at Gabrielle from between two low-slung branches. A foot stomped down, hard, on her instep. Startled, she tightened her grip on the scratchy bark.

Chin jutting out, a pint-size male face scowled at Gabrielle. "So put it back, you hear?" He wrapped stubby fingers around the branch nearest him and jiggled impatiently.

Needles spattered onto the soggy ground. "Me and my dad already chose *this* tree. It's *ours*. You gotta find another tree."

Not wanting to encourage the scamp, Gabrielle bit back her laughter and surveyed the small bundle of determination.

His shirt was carefully tucked into new blue jeans, his face was clean, and his eyes, dark brown and anxious, glared back at her. Someone had made a valiant attempt to slick down the cowlick at the crown of his head. The shoelaces on pricey new athletic shoes were double-tied.

Someone had taken pains to spiffy the boy up. Clearly, he didn't need her pity, but some thin edge of desperation or loneliness underneath his tenacity called to her.

Maybe it was only Christmas, the lights and smells of hope reaching out to her, making her vulnerable to this belligerent, wide-eyed waif. Or maybe it was her own loneliness and need for a perfect Christmas that shone back at her from this boy's eyes.

"So, lady, you understand? Right? You gotta find yourself another tree, okay?"

She heard the aggression, heard the rudeness. And in the soft darkness of a Florida night sweet-scented with pine and cinnamon and broken only by the glow of twinkling lights strung high from utility poles, she saw the bone-deep anxiety deepen in those eyes frowning up at her.

It was that anxiety and his dogged insistence that got to her. Bam. Like a hand reaching right into her chest, his need squeezed her heart.

But it was her damnable curiosity, which had been a besetting sin all her life, and maybe amusement that kept her interest as she watched him stiffen his shoulders and glower at her, waiting for her answer.

He was a pistol, he was, this tough little guy who wasn't about to give an inch just because she was bigger than he was. She took a deep breath. Somewhere in happy song land, elves were shrieking in glee because Santa had asked Rudolph to lead his sleigh. But here in Tibo's tree lot, as she stared at the pugnacious urchin, Gabrielle felt like the Grinch who was about to steal Christmas.

Wanting to erase that dread from his face, she dropped her hand. The tree wobbled, and she reached out to steady it. The boy's face scrunched in alarm as she grasped the tree again, and she released it as soon as she saw he was able to keep it upright. "How do you know I didn't see it first?" she asked, curious to see what he'd say.

"'Cause I was standing here guarding it. That's why." His not-Southern voice dripped with disbelief that she could be so dumb. He let part of the tree's weight rest against him. "My daddy's over there." Keeping his grip on the tree, the child jerked his chin toward the front of the lot. "He went to get Tibo. Tibo's gonna saw off the bottom so the tree can get enough water and last a-a-all Christmas," he said, finishing on a drawn-out hiss of excitement. "And in case you got any ideas, lady, you better not mess with my tree or with me 'cause my daddy's real tough. You'll be sorry," the boy said, never blinking. "You don't want to tangle with me and my daddy 'cause we're a team and we're tougher 'n a piece of old dried shoe leather."

"I see." Hearing the adult's voice in the childish treble, Gabrielle bit her lip to keep from smiling. "That's tough, all right."

"Da-*darned* straight." The square chin bobbed once, hard. "Nobody tangles with us. Not with me and my daddy, they don't, not if they know what's good for 'em." Sticking out his chest, he pulled his shoulders so far back that Gabrielle was afraid he'd pop a tendon.

This boy was definitely used to taking care of himself. His sturdy, small body fairly quivered with don't-mess-with-me attitude. Still, in spite of his conviction that he could handle anything, Gabrielle wasn't comfortable leaving him by himself. He couldn't be more than five, if that. Well, perhaps older, she thought, reconsidering the look in his eyes, but innocent for all his streetwise sass. And it was a scary world out there, even in Bayou Bend.

How could the father have walked off and left this child alone in the dark tree lot—in this day and age? It was none of her business, she knew, but she wouldn't be able to keep from telling the father that little guys shouldn't be left alone, not even in Tibo's tree lot.

"I'm sorry, but I really think I saw the tree first," she said, not caring about the tree, only trying to keep his attention while she scanned the empty aisles, looking for one tough daddy.

"Nope." He tipped his head consideringly but didn't move a hairbreadth from where he was standing.

"What, exactly, would your daddy do?" she asked, prolonging the moment and hoping the urchin's daddy would appear. "If I'd messed with—your tree?"

"Somethin'," her argumentative angel assured her. "Anyways, I know we seen it first. You was nowhere around."

"I saw this tree right away. I liked the shape of it." She fluffed a branch but made sure she didn't let her grasp linger as the boy's gaze followed her movement. "And it's big. I wanted a big tree this year." Her gaze lingered on the truly awful ugliness and bigness of the tree, and her voice caught. "I wanted a special tree."

He shifted, frowned and finally looked away from her, sighing as he glanced up at the tree. "Yeah. Me, too."

Again Gabrielle imagined she heard an underlying note of wistfulness in his froggy voice.

This stray had his reasons for choosing Tibo's sucker tree. She had hers.

The singing elves gave way to a jazzed-up "Jingle Bells," which boomed over her, and Gabrielle sighed. She and her dad had always made a point of dragging home the neediest tree they could find just to hear her mama rip loose with one of her musical giggles.

Last year, dazed and in a stupor, they had let Christmas become spring before either one of them climbed out of the pit they'd fallen into with her mama's death.

Christmas had always been Mary Kathleen O'Shea's favorite day.

Gabrielle and her dad hadn't been able to wrap their minds around the vision of that empty chair at the foot of the big dining room table. No way for either of them to fake a celebration, not with that image burned into their brains.

And so, in spite of a sixty-degree, bright blue Florida day that enticed Yankee tourists to dip a toe into the flat blue Gulf of Mexico, Christmas last year had been a cold, dark day in the O'Shea house.

This year, the giggles might once again be only a memory, but everything else was going to be the way it used to be. They'd have the right tree, the brightest lights strung on all the bushes around the old house, the flakiest mincemeat pie. Everything would be perfect. They'd find a way to deal with the empty chair, with all that it meant. In hindsight, she wondered if they shouldn't have forced themselves to face that emptiness last year, get past it. They hadn't, though, and the ache was as fresh as it had been barely a year ago.

But this Christmas, one way or another, was going to be perfect. Whatever perfect was, under the circumstances.

She sighed again and saw the boy's gaze flash to her face.

He shifted uneasily. "I'm sorry," he muttered, so softly she almost missed it. "But this is my special tree for me and my daddy."

She wanted to hug him, to wrap him in her arms and comfort him. Instead, knowing little boys, she tried for matter-of-fact.

"Well, that's life." Gabrielle thought she'd never heard a kid invoke daddy powers so often in so short a space of time. "Win some. Lose some," she said, hoping to erase the frown that still remained.

"Yeah. That's life," he repeated glumly before brightening. "Except at Christmas."

She heard the hope in his gruff treble. Well, why shouldn't it be there? All these Christmas lights strung up created a longing even in adults for magic, for *something* in this season when the world, even in Florida, seemed forever suspended in cold and darkness.

Her throat tightened, but she plunged ahead, desperate to change the direction of her thoughts. All this sighing and reminiscing weren't going to help her create her perfect Christmas.

"You didn't see me over by the fence? I was there, scoping out this very tree."

With his too-wise eyes, the boy examined her face, then shook his head with certainty. "Nah. You're trying to pull a fast one on me."

"Really?" The kid was too smart by half. "I might be telling the truth," she said thoughtfully, watching as he continued to study her face.

"Nope." He grinned, a flash of teeth showing in the twilight of the tree lot. "You're funning with me now."

Intrigued, she kneeled, going nose to nose with him. "How do you know?"

"I can tell." He shifted from one foot to the next, his attention wandering anxiously now from her to the front of the lot. "Grown-ups don't tell kids the truth. Not a lot, anyways."

"Oh." Gabrielle wrapped her arms around her knees to steady herself as she absorbed this truth from a kid who shouldn't have had time to learn it. "That's what you think I'm doing?"

"Sure." His mouth formed an upside-down U. "You're teasing me now, that's all."

This child had learned that his survival depended on knowing when the adults in his life were lying to him. She sensed he'd learned this truth in a hard school, that survival *had* depended on it. "You can tell when grown-ups are—funning with you?" She made her tone teasing.

"Funning's different from not telling the truth," he said matter-of-factly, his gaze drifting once more to the front of the lot. He, like her, was seeking the tough-but-absent daddy. "Funning's okay. No harm in funning. Most of the time."

"I see." Again that squeeze of her heart, that sharp pinch that made her catch her breath. "Want to draw straws for the tree?"

"No way," he scoffed. "You're still funning with me."

Suddenly delight washed over his face. "I remember! My daddy took the sticker off the tree, so we got proof."

"Ah. My loss, then." She smiled at him easily, letting him know their game was over.

In back of her, a foot scraped against one of the boards that formed narrow pathways between the aisles of trees. An elongated shadow slanted across her, and, still kneeling, still smiling back at the boy who'd shot her a quick grin, she pivoted, looking up at the silhouette looming above her.

"Daddy!" The boy wriggled from head to toe and launched himself at the silhouette, dragging the tree with him. "Daddy!"

Relieved, Gabrielle lifted her chin toward the tough daddy who'd finally shown up. Words formed on her lips—pleasant, instructive words designed to let this man know he should keep a closer eye on his son.

And then she saw the man's face.

Her heart lurched in her chest. Her throat closed, and her face flushed, with a heat so sudden and fierce she wondered she didn't burst into flames.

In front of her, Joe Carpenter, a lean, rangy male who'd been born with attitude to spare, attitude he'd apparently passed on to his son, rested his hand on the boy's shoulder and smiled gently down at the child who'd wrapped himself around his leg. "So, Oliver, reckon you're still determined to have this tree, huh?"

"Yeah." Clutching tree and man, the boy fastened one arm around Joe's waist and leaned against him. "This is the biggest tree. The best. A humdinger. *Our* tree. Right, huh?" He slanted a quick look at Gabrielle and before smiling blissfully at his father.

Gabrielle wondered if she could simply walk away, invisible, into the darkness, disappear behind tree branches, vanish. Anything so he wouldn't see her.

And then Joe Carpenter looked right at her, wicked amusement gleaming in weary brown eyes. "We've got to quit meeting like this, Gabby." He didn't smile, but the bayou brown of his eyes flashed with light and mischief.

As memory spun spiderwebs between them, she wished she were anywhere but kneeling at the feet of Joe Carpenter.

Knuckling his son's brown hair, hair only a few shades lighter than his own, Joe wrinkled his forehead. "Let me see. It's been what…?" One corner of his mouth gave a teeny-tiny twitch she almost missed in her embarrassment.

In spite of the past, a past embodied in Joe's son, a past made up of eleven years of creating her own life, she knew to the day and the month how long it had been. And he remembered, too, she decided as she watched his face and willed her own to fade from Christmas red to boring beige.

May 17. Saturday. Prom night. Out of place and miserable, she was fifteen years old and younger than her date's senior friends.

"Hey, pretty Gabby," he'd said that night, edging his motorcycle right up to the break wall behind the country club.

Water slapped against the dock while he surveyed her, the rumble of his cycle throbbing between them in the humid spring night.

"What are you doing out here? The dance is inside."

He motioned to the club behind them, with its faint bass beat and blaze of lights.

"I know." She turned her head and swiped away angry tears.

"So, you going to tell me why the prettiest girl is out here all by her lonesome? Or you going to make me guess?"

Gabrielle knew she wasn't the prettiest girl. She knew exactly who and what she was. She was the *good* girl, the one who chaired school committees, worked on the homecoming floats, went to church every Sunday. The girl everybody could count on. The girl who took everything too seriously.

Oh, she knew what she was. She wasn't the prettiest girl, not by anybody's definition, but she liked being precisely who she was, and now Joe Carpenter was teasing her, or making fun of her, or flirting with her. Whatever he was doing, she didn't know how to respond, and she wanted him to stop.

But she wanted even more for him to keep talking to her in that deliciously husky voice that raised the hairs on her arms.

That deep voice vibrated inside her, creating a hunger so unfamiliar that she felt like someone else, not a bit like Gabrielle O'Shea.

Joe Carpenter made her feel—wild.

And curious.

So she drew up her knees under the pale chiffon of her slim skirt, tried not to sniff too loudly and stared out at the shimmer of moonlight on the water. Better to watch the glisten of the water than to think about what Joe Carpenter might mean, because good girls knew better than to be alone with Joe. Even if they wanted to.

Even when their bodies hummed to the tuning fork of Joe Carpenter's voice.

Especially then, she decided, and wrapped herself tighter in her own arms.

He waited for a moment, but when she stayed silent, he kicked down the motorcycle stand, turned off the engine and walked over to her, his boots squeaking against the wet grass. "The prettiest girl should be inside, dancing the last dance. The one where they finally turn down the lights real low and everybody snuggles up and pretends all that touchin' is accidental."

Thinking about the kind of touching he meant, she shivered, and her barely there breasts tingled interestingly.

His voice burred with a kind of teasing she wasn't able to return, and he stepped nearer. "You know what I mean, Gabby. The kissing dance. That's what you're missing. I bet

Johnny Ray's looking all over for you. He'd want to dance real slow, real close, and see if your hair smells as pretty as it looks.''

He flicked his half-smoked cigarette into the bay and took one more step closer, his thighs bumping her stockinged toes. "Because I've been wondering. Does it, Gabby? Does it smell like rain shine and night jasmine?" With the tip of his finger, he brushed the top of her head, and her toes curled hard against the cement break wall.

She didn't say a word. Couldn't. Not even when he ran one callused finger down her shoulder, slipping under the cap sleeve of her dress and tracing the veins of her inner arm. She didn't speak even when he touched her wrist, gently, lightly, a butterfly touch that made her pulse skip and stutter. With a half smile she would wonder about for years, he lifted her arm, holding it up. Moonlight glinted on the thin band of her bracelet, on her skin, turning everything silver.

"Aw, what the hell," he muttered. "Johnny Ray's not here, but I am. Too bad for ol' Johnny Ray," he said, and tucked her arm around his neck. "Damned if I'm not going to find out for myself what rain shine smells and tastes like." His gaze never leaving hers, he lifted one of the curls that had cost her thirty-five dollars at Sally Lynn's salon and, shutting his eyes, stroked the curl against his mouth. "Delicious, that's what," he whispered, his dark eyes filling her sight. "Who could have guessed?"

And then the baddest of the bad boys kissed her, and she kissed him right back, a great big smooch of a kiss, tongues and lips and bodies touching in that silvery light. Oh, Lord, the touching. All down the stretch of his tough, hard body, her fifteen-year-old self melted, and there had been touching.

She liked feeling wild and wicked and out of control. She liked the hum of her body against his, liked the powerful drumming of his heart against her hand.

But just when she felt like soda pop fizzing out of control, his breath buzzing into her ear and making her insides quiver, he'd murmured, "You may be jailbait, sweet pea, but I swear to God it would be worthwhile. Except—"

He pushed her away from him, leaving her skin cold and hot and aching all at the same time. Stepping away with a grin that promised heaven or hell—she'd never been able to decide—he straddled his cycle and left her in a squeal of tires against pavement while she tried to decide if she wanted to call her daddy to come and pick her up or steal the car keys from her football-hero, drunk-as-a-skunk prom date.

For the rest of that night, her mouth, her body, her skin— *everything*—had ached and burned with that cold heat, and for the next two years she'd dreamed about Joe Carpenter.

Of course, she hadn't seen him again after that night.

He'd vanished, leaving Bayou Bend with its own kind of buzz as rumors floated, eddied and finally died away, leaving unexplained the mystery of nineteen-year-old Joe Carpenter's disappearance one month shy of graduation.

Now, staring up the length of his legs and thighs, Gabrielle swallowed. Even in the darkness of this Christmas tree lot, eleven years later, her entire body flushed with that memory.

No wonder he'd been the town's bad boy.

Well, she didn't want those disturbing dreams haunting her again. It had taken too many sleepless nights, too many confused days for her to erase Joe Carpenter from her dreams, her memories.

"So how long *has* it been?" he asked, his voice low and rumbly, goading, baiting her. "Let me think if I can remember the last time I saw you, Gabby. It must have been—"

"A while," she said grimly, struggling to her feet and catching one flat-heeled shoe on slippery needles and mud. "That's how long. A while." Her foot skidded forward and her arms windmilled crazily. Flailing, she saw her purse sail into the darkness.

"Whoa, sweet pea." Joe's warm hand closed around her elbow and braced her, his still-callused fingers sliding down her wrist as she balanced.

Even through the silk of her blouse, Gabrielle felt that warm, rough slide. His hand had been warm that night, too, warm against her bare skin. She shivered.

"Cold?" Amusement glittered in his eyes. Heat was in the depths, too, as he watched her.

He knew what he was doing, as he had eleven years ago, eleven years that had vanished like smoke with his touch. He knew, but she was darned if she'd give him the satisfaction of going all giddy and girlish.

She was twenty-six years old, too old for girlish. Giddy and girlish had never been her style, not even at fifteen. "It's the damp. That's all," she muttered. "I'm not used to it anymore."

"Sure that's all it is?" His question, below the raucous rendition of the chipmunks and their version of "Jingle Bells," tickled the edge of her cheek where he bent over her, still supporting her.

"Absolutely."

"You moved away from Bayou Bend?" He clamped a hand under her elbow and steadied her.

"I've been living in Arizona. Same rattlesnakes. Less humid." She dusted off her red velour skirt, shot Oliver a smile and a "so long" and slung her shoulder strap over her arm. "Nice to see you again, Joe. Merry Christmas to you and your son."

She was almost safe. One second more, and she would have been up the walkway and gone, out to her car, away from the slamming of her heart against her chest, away from memory and the sizzle of his touch. One second. That's all she needed.

Out of the darkness of the next aisle, Moon Tibo lumbered, bumping into her and pitching her straight into Joe Carpenter's arms. "Okay, folks, let's haul this tree up front and get you on your way. I mean, you only got twenty-four days to the big event. Y'all gonna want time to hang up them ornaments before this year's over, right?''

"Right." Joe's laugh gusted against her ear, and Gabrielle felt her toes curl in memory. "Give me a minute, Moon. Got a damsel in distress here.''

"Oh, yeah. Sure. How ya doin', Gabrielle? Your dad feelin' better?''

"Much." She was all tied up with her purse strap and Joe's arms, and she twisted, pushed, while Joe's chest shook with laughter against her. Over its broad slope, she finally angled her face in Moon's direction. "Dad's cooking jambalaya tomorrow night, in fact. For after we decorate the tree. Come on over. He'd enjoy seeing you.''

Six foot five and built like a mountain, Moon gifted her with one of his rare smiles. "Might do that. Sure like your dad, I do.''

She tugged again at her strap, which had flicked over Joe's head and bound them together. Mumbling under her breath to Joe, whose only help so far had been to keep her from landing face first in pine needles and mud, she said, "Give me a hand, will you? I can't do this alone.''

"You got it, sweet pea. Lots of things aren't any fun done alone. I like lending a helping hand." His half smile could have lit up the town of Bayou Bend for a couple of blocks, and even Gabrielle's forehead blazed with heat. Lifting the strap, he ducked under it, his thick hair brushing up against her mouth, and stepped back. "I'm ready to help out. When I can." His palm was flat and firm against the hollow of her spine. "How's that?''

"Peachy. Thanks." Gabrielle untangled herself from Joe's clasp and brushed back her hair. Joe Carpenter would flirt if he were wrapped up like an Egyptian mummy. "This has been—special.''

"Absolutely." He plucked a pine needle twig from her hair

and handed it to her. "A memento, Gabby. For old times' sake." His voice was light, amused, and his eyes teased her.

But behind the gleam, deep in their shadowy depths, she thought—no, imagined—she saw regret, a regret that made no sense, and so, surely, she must be imagining that rueful glint.

"We never had old times, Joe." She mustered a smile and let the twig fall to the ground.

"No?"

She shook her head and hoped her own regret didn't break through. "Not me. You must be thinking of someone else." Anyone else, she reminded herself. Joe's track record with adolescent hearts in high school had been gold-medal worthy.

But if she were honest with herself, and she tried to be, she knew her regret ran ocean deep because she'd never, ever felt that wildness with anyone since. She wasn't fifteen anymore, and she could handle Joe Carpenter's teasing. Sure she could, she thought as his eyes narrowed intently for a moment.

"Well. If you say so. Must not have been you I was re-membering outside the country club." He shrugged and let his hand rest on Oliver's head. "It was real good seeing you again." His gaze sharpened as he gave her a last glance. "Nice, that red skirt and silky blouse." He smiled, and again that flicker of regret appeared in his eyes. "You look like a shiny Christmas present, Gabby."

The weariness unraveling his voice and slumping his shoulders was real, and she hesitated, knowing she was making a mistake, knowing she'd be a fool to open her mouth when she had her exit line handed to her on a plate. Say goodbye and walk away. That's all she had to do.

She opened her mouth, then closed it. She would be asking for more trouble than she wanted, needed. And then, looking down at the boy, Joe's son, she spoke. "Come for supper. Tomorrow night." Joe's sudden stillness told him the invitation surprised him as much as it did her.

She would have taken the words back, but they hung in the

air, an invitation she hadn't intended, an invitation she wished she could take back the minute she spoke.

"Why doncha, Joe? Milo sure wouldn't care. You know how he is. More the merrier, that's what ol' Milo says." Moon hoisted the tree up with one hand and strode up the aisle toward the shed where the trees were trimmed and netted.

Gabrielle stared after him. She might have known, Moon being Moon, he would stick his two cents in. Trapped, she added politely for appearances' sake, "Dad makes a big pot. He wouldn't mind."

"Jambalaya, huh?" Joe rubbed his chin. "Milo makes good jambalaya."

"How would you know?" She closed her mouth, stunned. To the best of her knowledge, despite Moon's blithe assertion, Joe Carpenter had never met her father.

"Oh, I've had a plate or two of your pa's cooking." Running a hand through his hair, Joe glanced at Oliver, back to her, and then said, so slowly she couldn't believe what she was hearing, "Thanks. I reckon we'll take you up on your offer. It's a good idea."

Oliver, who'd been strangely silent throughout the whole incident, glared up at her, his face as fierce as it had been the first time she'd seen him, but he didn't say anything. Taking a sideways step, he plastered himself against his father and stayed there, a scowling barnacle to Joe's anchor.

Uneasiness rippled through Gabrielle as she saw the boy's hostility return, and she wished, not for the first time in her life, that she'd counted to ten before speaking. She was trapped, though, caught by Moon's interference.

Judging by the expression on his face, Oliver was trapped, too. As she looked away from his frown, her words tumbled out. "Good. Company will be great. That's what the season is all about. Family, friends. Get-togethers. Eggnog." Mumbling, Gabrielle scrabbled through her purse for a piece of paper and a pen.

"Right." The corner of Joe's mouth twitched. "Eggnog's always sort of summed up Christmas for me." He ruffled his son's hair. "Eggnog do it for you, Oliver?"

"No." Oliver worked his scowl into a truly awesome twist of mouth and nose. "Eggnog stinks."

Joe's hand stilled on the boy's head. "Mind your manners, Oliver," he said softly and then spoke to Gabrielle. "We'll be there."

Restraining her impulsive nature, she bit her bottom lip. Her instinct was to reassure Oliver, but faced with his ferocious grimace, she stopped. Oliver's likes and dislikes were Joe's concern, not hers.

Even though the boy's anger was clearly directed toward her, she knew enough about kids not to take it personally. She didn't know anything about this particular child. Whatever was going on between him and his father would have to be settled between them. She wasn't involved.

She pulled out a small cork-covered pad and flipped it open. "All right, then. Let me write out the address."

"I know where you live, Gabby." Joe's hand covered hers, and yearning pierced her, as sweet and poignant as the smell of pine on the cool evening air.

It was all she could do not to turn up her palm and link her fingers with his.

"Unless you've moved?"

"No." Her voice sounded strangled even to her own ears. "Dad hasn't moved." Unnerved by the thought that he knew where she lived, she flicked the notebook shut, open. "Oh," she said, dismayed as a sudden thought struck her. She looked up, made herself meet his gaze straight on. "And bring your wife, too. As Moon said, Dad likes a crowd."

"I'm not married, Gabby." Joe's bare ring finger passed in front of her. He closed her notebook, his hand resting against the brown cork. "What time?"

"What?" Her mind went blank. Nothing made sense. Joe

Carpenter, the Harley-Davidson-riding outlaw who could seduce with a look, had a son. Joe Carpenter knew her dad.

Joe Carpenter, whose kiss could melt steel and a young girl's heart, was coming to her house for jambalaya and tree trimming.

And eggnog.

Sometime when she wasn't paying attention, hell must have frozen over.

Even in Bayou Bend, Florida.

Chapter Two

"The time, Gabby?" The tip of Joe's finger tapped gently against her chin, snapping her out of her bemusement.

"What time shall Oliver and I come caroling at your door?"

"Eight, I suppose. That might be late for your son, though." She hoped Joe would pick up the hint and let her off the hook.

Joe Carpenter, of course, didn't. "Not a problem. Oliver doesn't start school until after the holidays."

Gabby sighed, a tiny exhalation. Joe had a plan. She couldn't imagine what was possessing him to take her up on her invitation, an invitation offered only out of politeness, not for any other reason.

Liar, liar. You like being around Joe.

With a jerk of her head, she silenced the snide little voice and dislodged Joe's finger. Her chin tingled, as if that phantom touch lingered warm against her skin.

Bearlike in his red-and-green plaid shirt, Moon waited for them to join him. "Well, then, you folks ready to check out?"

He held up a red plastic ball made of two hoops and topped with mistletoe and a green yarn bow. "Free kissing ball with each tree." Moon wagged the kissing ball in front of her until she thought her eyes would cross.

Resolutely, she kept her gaze fixed on the tip of Moon's Santa hat and told herself she was merely imagining the heat lapping at her, washing from Joe to her, and wrapping her in warmth and thoughts of more than kissing.

"Somethin' special for old Moon's customers, this is. And we got treats in the shed. Cookies. Apple cider. The boy can have a cup of hot chocolate while I bundle up this beauty. So come along, y'all." A trail of brown needles followed Moon's progress as he herded them forward. "Good stuff, cocoa. You'd like that, wouldn't you, young fella?"

Oliver ducked before Moon's beefy hand landed on his head. "Maybe. Maybe not." He trudged after Moon and the tree.

Moon grinned back. "Shucks, kid. Everybody likes hot chocolate."

Oliver planted one new shoe after the other, following Moon and hanging one hand tight to the edge of Joe's pocket. "I only like it the way my daddy makes it. Out of the brown can and stirred on the stove. And only with little marshmallows." Head down, ignoring Moon, Oliver adjusted his shorter stride to Joe's, matching left foot to left.

The boy needed physical contact with his father. Gabrielle slowed and let the two of them walk slightly ahead of her, a team, just as the boy had stressed. Everybody else on the outside.

Her curiosity stirred again as she watched the two, one rangy and dark, a lean length of man, the other, short and dark, a stubby child with eyes only for his father.

"Where's your tree, Gabby?" Joe stopped and looked over his shoulder at her. "Oliver and I'll give you a hand with it while Moon bundles ours."

"Umm." She saw something tall and green from the corner of her eye and pointed. "That one."

"That one?" Not believing her, Joe stared at the ratty tree. The one Oliver had insisted on was three good shakes away from mulch, but Gabby's tree— "You sure?" He frowned at her. "This one is, uh, well—"

"It's a terrific tree. It'll look wonderful with all the old ornaments." Gabby tilted her face up at him. Her off-center smile filled her face. Christmas lights sparkled in her mist-dampened soft brown hair, and he wanted to touch that one spot near her cheek where a strand fluttered with the breeze against her neck.

The look of her at that moment, all shiny and sweet and innocently hopeful, symbolized everything he'd come back to find in Bayou Bend, a town he'd hated and couldn't wait to leave. Like the star at the top of a Christmas tree, Gabby sparkled like a beacon in the darkness of Moon's tree lot.

"Come on, Daddy. We got to go." Oliver pulled anxiously on his hand.

Still watching the glisten of lights in the mass of her brown hair, Joe cleared his suddenly thick throat. "Right. But we'll help Gabby first, Oliver. Because we're stronger."

"She don't need our help. Moon can wrap her tree."

"Mr. Tibo to you, squirt."

"She looks strong enough to me." Oliver scowled and kicked at the ground.

Joe scanned Gabby's slight form, the gentle curves of her hips under some red, touch-me, feel-me material, the soft slope of her breasts beneath her blouse, breasts that trembled with her breath as she caught his glance. His gaze lingering on her, he spoke to his son. "Well, maybe she is strong in spite of the fact that she looks like a good sneeze would tip her over. Let's say helping out's a neighborly kind of thing to do, okay?"

"Neighbors?"

He would have sworn her breathy voice feathered right down each vertebra under his naked skin. Even as a teenager, her voice had had that just-climbed-out-of-bed sigh. He wondered if she knew its effect on males.

Her voice was the first thing he'd noticed about her back when he'd moved to Bayou Bend as a surly high school troublemaker.

Even then, the soft breathiness of Gabby O'Shea's voice held something sweet and kind that soothed the savage creature raging inside him.

Seeing him on the sidewalk outside the grocery store where he'd lied his way into a part-time job, she'd smiled at him in his black leather jacket and tight jeans and said, "Hi, Joe Carpenter. Welcome to Bayou Bend." Her voice slid over the syllables and held him entranced even as he folded his arms and gave her a distant, disinterested nod.

At seventeen, a year older than his classmates and new to this small community, cool Joe Carpenter didn't have time to waste on thirteen-year-old skinny girls with kind voices, not when high school girls fell all over one another offering to give him anything he wanted. Thirteen-year-old junior high girls were off-limits, not worth wasting time on.

But, touching that bitter, angry place he'd closed off to the world, her voice made him remember her over the next two years as she grew into a young woman, made him lift his head in baffled awareness whenever he heard that soft voice reminding him all the world wasn't hard and mean and nasty.

And now, even years after he'd fled Bayou Bend, her voice sent his pulse into overdrive with its just-got-out-of-bed breathiness.

"We're going to be neighbors?"

He shook his head, clearing his thoughts as she repeated her question. "Yeah, Gabby. All of us. You. Me. Oliver. We're going to be neighbors. I bought the Chandlers' house. Down the block from your place."

"Oh." Her hair whipped against his shoulder, tangled in the fabric of his jacket, pulled free as she turned toward the tree she'd chosen. "I hadn't heard." With two hands, she lifted her tree and thumped it up and down on the ground a couple of times.

He could have driven a pickup truck through the spaces between the branches, but at least her tree didn't drop needles like a cry for help.

"We're living in a hotel." Oliver tugged him toward Gabby's tree and checked it out critically. "For now. With a indoor swimming pool. I like the hotel."

"You're going to have a tree in the hotel?" Gabby's quick glance at him was puzzled. "That's nice, but—"

"A friend's letting us store the tree for a day or two. We're moving into our house on Tuesday." Joe watched as her eyes widened, flicked away from his.

"Ah." She touched the branch. "Tuesday. You'll be busy. Do you need some—" She stopped, just as she had before she'd issued her invitation.

Help was what he thought she almost offered before she caught herself.

She was uneasy with him. Edgy. Aware of him.

He took a deep breath. Nice, that awareness.

With one hand still wrapped around Joe's, Oliver poked his head under one of the branches. "This is a okay tree. Not as good as ours, though."

Joe inhaled, ready to scold Oliver, to say something, anything, because the kid had a mouth on him. But then Gabby's laughing hazel eyes stopped him. Her mouth was all pursed up as if she was about to bust out laughing. He shrugged.

"No problem. And Oliver's right." She gasped as his son glowered at her. "His tree *is* better. In fact, a few minutes earlier, we were negotiating which one of us was going to walk away with it." Her expression told him not to sweat the small stuff.

At least that's what he thought it meant.

"Right, Oliver?"

"We didn't nogosh—didn't do that thing you said," his son, stubborn as ever, insisted. "It was my tree 'cause I seen it first. Me and her settled that."

"Yes, we did," Gabby confirmed, smiling down at Oliver.

Joe ran a hand through his hair. Should he make Oliver give up their tree to Gabby? Was that the right thing to do? Hell, what did he know? He was the last person to try and teach a kid about manners and being a good neighbor and—

This daddy business didn't come with instructions. Wasn't like putting a bicycle together. More like flying by the seat of your pants, he was beginning to see. He didn't think he'd ever get the hang of it.

And he wasn't used to having a small recorder around, copying his words, imitating his ways, watching everything he did.

The responsibility made him lie awake at night, his blood running cold with the sure knowledge that he wasn't father material, while Oliver's warm neck rested against the crook of his arm.

"I like this tree, Joe," Gabby said gently, as if she could read his thoughts.

Her voice warmed the chill creeping through him. Scrubbing his scalp hard, he stopped his spinning thoughts. "Fine, Gabby. If that's the one you want."

"Oh, it definitely is." Her laugh rippled through the air. "It will be absolutely perfect for Dad and me."

"Whatever you say. Come on, Oliver. You take that branch and haul it up to your shoulder."

"'Course." His son puffed out a biceps you could almost see without a microscope. "Because I'm strong."

"I can see you really are," Gabby said admiringly, her expression tender as she looked down at his grumpy son.

God. His son.

Once more that weight settled over him. The responsibility. The constant fear that he'd mess up. But he'd asked for this responsibility, gone looking for it, in fact. He would do what he had to do.

"Ready, Oliver?" Joe heaved the tree off its temporary stand.

"Sure." Oliver clamped onto the assigned branch with both hands. "This is easy." His whole body was hidden by the branch held tightly in his grip.

"Can you see?" Gabby's question brought Oliver's attention back to her.

"I can see my daddy's behind."

"A guiding light, huh? So to speak."

This time Joe was sure he heard a strangled laugh underneath her words.

"Watch it, smarty-pants," he muttered to her as she walked beside Oliver. "Nothing good happens to smart alecks."

"Who? Me?" Her hair glittered and glistened, shimmered with her movements in the damp air.

"Oh, sure. You have that butter-won't-melt-in-your-mouth look to you, Gabby. Even in eighth grade, you looked as if you were headed straight for the convent. Still do, in fact." He lifted one eyebrow and felt satisfaction as her face flamed pink. "But I know better. That nifty red skirt gives you away, you know. That skirt's an invitation to sin, sweet pea."

She sped up her steps, trying to pass him.

"You're wicked, Gabby, that's what you are." He liked the flustered look she threw him. "Wicked Gabby with the innocent eyes and bedroom voice."

Her mouth fell open even as she danced to his other side.

He liked keeping her off balance. One of these days, if he ever had the time, he'd have to figure out why he liked pushing her buttons. Always had. "You're a bad girl, Gabby." He waggled a finger in a mock scold. "Santa's not coming down your chimney this year, I'll bet."

"Oh, stop it, you fool," she sputtered, finally darting past him with a laugh. "You're incorrigible, Joe, that's what *you* are."

"Shoot, everybody knows that."

"What's corgibull?" Oliver planted his feet firmly in place, stopping the procession. He stuck his head up from behind the branch. "And why are you and her laughing? What's so funny?"

"Your daddy is funning with me. He's making *very* inappropriate jokes," Gabby said primly, digging in her wallet and sending Joe a sideways scolding look as she dragged out money for the tree.

"Yeah?" Oliver stuck his fist on a nonexistent hip and rushed to Joe's defense. "My daddy's 'propriate."

"Oliver's right, Gabby." Joe tightened his mouth. "I'm very appropriate. Especially—"

"Uncle," she said, her eyes gleaming with laughter and something else that made Joe want to step closer and see for himself what shifted in the depths of those changeable eyes.

But he didn't.

Getting too close to Gabrielle O'Shea would be one of the stupidest moves in a lifetime filled with mistakes.

"I give up, Joe. Let me pay for this dratted tree and get home. Dad's probably wondering what sinkhole opened up and swallowed me."

Joe stood the tree against a pole.

Pine needles in his hair and all over his clothes, Oliver stomped up beside him.

"Stay with Gabby, Oliver, while I lug this tree over to Moon."

Mutiny glowered back at him.

"It's polite, son. To provide ladies with an escort." Feeling like a fool, Joe didn't dare look at Gabby. She'd be laughing her head off at him. Him. Giving etiquette lessons to a kid. What on earth was the world coming to?

When he turned around, though, she wasn't laughing. Her

face had gone all blurry and kissable, and he couldn't figure out what he'd done to make her look at him the way she was.

If they'd been alone, he would have kissed her for sure. Would have stepped right up to her, wrapped his arms around her narrow waist and given in to the itch to see what that shiny blouse felt like under his hands.

No question about it. He wanted to kiss her more than he'd wanted anything for himself in a long while.

Instead, ignoring the warning alarms in his brain, the voice screeching *Stupid! Stupid!* he gave in to the lesser temptation and slicked back the curl of hair that had been tantalizing him for the last fifteen minutes.

Against the back of his hand, her hair was slippery like the silk of her blouse. Against his palm, the slim column of her neck was night-and-mist cool. For a long moment she stood there, not moving, just breathing, hazel eyes turning a rich, deep green, jewels shining in the darkness as she stared at him. He curled his palm around her nape and dipped his head.

Well, he'd never laid claim to sainthood.

Against the end of his finger, her pulse fluttered and sang to him, a siren call.

And beside him, clinging like a limpet, his son leaned, small and cranky and utterly dependent on him.

The strains of "O Holy Night" drifted to him. Heated by her body and nearness, the scent of Gabby, so close, so close, rose to him. Surrounded by scent and sound, he forgot everything except the woman in front of him.

Forgot the silenced alarms in his brain.

Forgot responsibility.

Forgot *everything*.

Oliver pulled at the edge of Joe's pocket. "I want to go, Daddy. I'm tired."

Joe stepped back and let his hand fall to his side. He wasn't about to tell sweet Gabby he was sorry, because he wasn't, not at all. If it wasn't for Oliver, well, mistake or not, he'd have Gabby O'Shea wrapped up against him tighter than plastic wrap.

But Oliver was in his life with needs and fears Joe was only beginning to glimpse.

His son had taken up permanent residence in the cold, lonely recesses of Joe's heart.

No one else had ever found the key to that cramped room. But Oliver had, that first time three weeks ago when Joe had taken his small hand in his and walked with Oliver out of the apartment where he'd been left.

Not hesitating, Oliver had picked up a raggedy blanket, latched onto Joe's hand and said only, "I told Suzie you'd come. I told her I had a daddy who would find me." He'd smiled at Joe, a funky, trusting, gap-toothed smile. "I knowed you would. You did."

That had been that.

Next to that power, even Gabby in Christmas mist and glittery lights could be resisted.

He hoped. And maybe only because she backed away at the same time he did, both of them knowing better than to yield to that sizzle.

So when his son's gruff voice came again, Joe knew the choice was easy. Whatever he wanted wasn't a drop in the bucket compared with what Oliver needed.

It couldn't be.

He wouldn't let anybody, not even himself, cause this tiny scrap of humanity one more second's worth of pain.

"Okay, squirt. You're right. It's late. But first we have to drop off Gabby's tree with Moon. Then we'll hit the highway. We'll decide what to do about the party later."

Oliver's sigh was heavy enough to crush rocks. "I want to go home. *Now*. And I don't want to go to a party."

Joe was torn. What was he supposed to do? Yell at the kid for being mouthy? Is that what a good parent would do? It didn't feel right, though, not with Oliver looking up at him

like a damned scared puppy who'd just peed on the rug. Hell.
Strangled, Joe tugged at his shirt collar.

Gabby curled her fingers around Joe's arm. "No problem,
Joe. You and Oliver decide after you get back to the hotel
whether you want to stop at the house tomorrow night. Right
now, Oliver's tired and probably hungry." Not crowding his
son, she added casually, "Maybe having some of Moon's cocoa and doughnuts would be a good idea."

Her skirt pulled tight across the delicate curves of her fanny
as she stooped to Oliver's level, her manner easy and relaxed.
Joe admired the way she gave Oliver space.

He admired her tidy curves, too, and decided a man could
be forgiven for appreciating a work of nature. Looking didn't
hurt anyone. Be a shame not to admire Gabby's behind. After
all, she'd checked out his.

She caught his faint grin and yanked her skirt free where it
had tightened against her.

"Turnabout's fair play," he drawled. "And the view is
swell."

Being a woman of good sense, she ignored him. "Oliver, I
understand you're particular about your cocoa. Anybody
would be, but Moon makes a killer cup of chocolate. The older
guys like it. But maybe it's an acquired taste." She stood up,
shrugged. "You'd make Moon feel good if you gave his cocoa
the Oliver taste test."

His son hesitated, reluctant to give in. Stubborn little squirt.
"Maybe I'll take a sip. If it'll make Moon feel better."

Bless her. Oliver *was* probably hungry. Joe kept forgetting
how fast a six-year-old ran out of gas.

"I was thinking—" Gabby wrinkled up her face "—that
you look like a guy with discriminating taste buds."

Intrigued, Oliver quit scuffing the ground.

"Doughnuts might not be your thing. Want to try some trail
mix?" Gabby pulled out a plastic bag with chips of dried fruit

and nuts. Opening the closure, she pulled out a couple of raisins and offered the bag to Joe.

"Trail mix sounds good. Raisins, huh?" Joe hated raisins, hated dried fruit. Prissy stuff. But he took a handful and handed the bag to Oliver, who, imitating him, grabbed a fistful and shoveled it into his mouth.

"Lots of raisins." A sly smile tugged at Gabby's mouth, curving her full bottom lip up. "You like raisins, don't you, Joe?"

"Yum. My favorite—" Dubiously he looked at the wrinkled speck he held between two fingers.

"Fruit, Joe. Filled with nutrition." Her eyes sparkled up at him.

"Yeah. I know." He ate a raisin and figured he'd learned another lesson. Carry food. He reckoned his jackets would start looking like chipmunk cheeks before the kid grew up.

No wonder kids needed two parents. His respect for single parents shot up five hundred notches. How did they do it, day after day? How could *he* be this kid's only adult? Day after day.

Impossible.

He scowled.

"Hope your face doesn't freeze like that, Joe." Gabby poked him in the stomach.

"I was just thinking."

"Oh?" The sweetness in her voice almost undid him.

"Nothing." Grimly, he picked up the tree and walked to the shed, Gabby slightly ahead of him. Clamped at his side, Oliver chomped happily on trail mix.

The kid deserved better than a selfish thirty-year-old loner who didn't have a clue what he was supposed to do now that he'd become a parent literally overnight.

You couldn't return a child like a piece of merchandise.

A kid was for life.

The kid hadn't asked for Joe, either, not really. Oliver had wished on a star for a dad, and a whimsical fate had thrown him Joe.

So, the kid was stuck with him as a dad. Joe was all the kid had. Where was the fairness in that? The justice?

Coming to the end of the aisle of trees, Joe tipped his head up to the velvet blackness of night in Bayou Bend. Nothing in the star-spangled darkness answered him. Sighing, he glanced back down at his son.

And in that moment, as he watched Oliver manfully chew on trail mix while checking out Joe's reaction, wonder settled over Joe. Nobody had ever looked at him like that, like he'd hung the moon and stars, like their whole world was filled with him.

He might be all the kid had, he might not be worth a tinker's damn as a father, but, by heaven, he had one thing working for him.

He wanted to do right by this boy more than he'd ever wanted anything in his life. That ought to count for something.

Taking a deep breath, Joe grinned at Oliver. "Come on. Hitch a ride on an old hoss." Holding the tree with one hand, he swung Oliver up onto his shoulders and settled him. "Been a long day, huh, partner?" He patted Oliver's foot.

Oliver rested his chin on top of Joe's head as they approached the shed. "Yeah." Oliver's chin ground into Joe's head with each munch of trail mix. "I like it up here." He folded both arms on top of Joe's head and wrapped his legs around Joe's neck.

Hell, nobody was born knowing how to be a parent. There were plenty of books on the subject. Joe could learn. He'd make mistakes, but he could keep from making the same mistake twice. With a little luck.

And a lot of work.

He could do this daddy business.

"I'll find Moon, Joe. If you don't mind, just lean the tree against the shed and you two go have that cup of cocoa."

Gabby reached up and wiggled Oliver's toe. "Nice meeting you, Oliver. Let me know what you think of Moon's cocoa, hear?" She pivoted and whisked behind the corner of the shed so fast Joe didn't have a chance to stop her.

He thought the night seemed darker and colder without the glow of Gabby's face.

"Let's go, Daddy." Leaning forward, Oliver peered into Joe's face. "We don't need anybody else, do we?"

"Duck, son. The shed door's low." He didn't see Gabby again. By the time he and Oliver drank cocoa, checked out the baskets of ornaments and made their way to the van, Gabby was nowhere in sight.

"Gabby leave yet?" Joe slammed the van door shut.

"Right after I tied down her trunk. She was in a hurry. Worried about her dad, I guess."

"Milo looked fine when I saw him. But that was from a distance." Joe lifted Oliver into the passenger side and motioned for him to fasten the seat belt. "What's the problem?"

"Damned if I know. Milo's complaining about Gabrielle coming home, swearing she's making a fuss over nothing, that's all I know. He's worked up a head of steam about Gabrielle threatening to sell her Arizona condo and come back to Bayou Bend on a permanent basis." Moon leaned over confidentially. "You ask me—and I notice you didn't—that's the problem."

"I don't get it. What do you mean?" Sticking the key into the ignition switch, Joe paused. "She's back for good?"

"That's what's making Milo crazy. He's ranting and raving that she would be making a mistake, that he doesn't need any help—"

"Does he?" Joe straightened out Oliver's twisted seat belt and snapped it into the slot.

"I don't know." Moon rolled his shoulders. "He was in the hospital for three weeks back around Halloween, but you know Milo."

"No, actually, I don't. Not well, anyway."

"Huh." Moon raised his eyebrows. "Funny. I thought you knew the old man. Don't know where I got that idea."

"Neither do I." Joe kept his face empty of expression. What Moon might know or might guess wasn't important. Joe wasn't about to fill him in on any details.

He'd told Moon the truth. He didn't know Milo well.

Not in the usual meaning, at least.

Moon nodded. "Anyway, if Milo's got a health problem, he sure wouldn't broadcast it. He'd make a joke out of it, but he'd keep any problem to himself. Milo's good at keeping secrets."

Joe didn't have to be a rocket scientist to read between the lines. Moon knew something, after all, about that night years ago, but, like Milo, he could keep a secret. "Thanks for your help, Moon." Joe reached out to shake Moon's ham-size hand.

Moon's face split into a grin. "Sure. Any old time." His squeeze of Joe's hand was hard enough to discourage circulation for a few minutes. As Joe started to pull the driver's door shut, Moon rested his hand on it, stopping Joe's movement. All the folksy drawl disappeared from Moon's rumble of a voice as he gave Joe a keen look and said, "Merry Christmas to you and your boy." He slammed the van door shut. "And, Joe…"

"Yeah?"

"Welcome home."

Looking at Moon's large, sincere face, where understanding lay beneath the good-old-boy mask, Joe felt his throat close up.

He'd felt the same way years ago when Gabby welcomed him to Bayou Bend, a place he'd never called home.

A place he couldn't wait to run from as fast as he could.

A place he'd returned to because of Oliver.

And if it killed him, he was going to make this town home for his son.

Staying away from Gabrielle O'Shea would be part of that price, no matter how drawn he was to her sweetness.

In the hotel later, Joe watched shadows dance across the wall. Shifting, changing, like his life, the shadows passed one after another, each blurring into the other until the original pattern was no longer visible.

Beside him, snoring gently, small bubbles popping with each breath, his son slept. Peacefully. Securely.

Safely.

For the first time since he'd heard about his son, a son he didn't even know he had, Joe slept soundly, too.

In his dreams, pine scent and Christmas carols mingled, and he followed the glow of Gabby's smile, like a star leading him through the darkness.

Chapter Three

"Here. Taste." Milo handed Gabrielle a wooden spoon dripping with broth and rice. "What do you think?"

Gabrielle thought her dad's face was too gray and too exhausted-looking, that's what she thought. She kept her opinion to herself and took the spoon. Tasted. A complex mix of flavors burst on her tongue, and she sighed with pleasure. Her dad's version of jambalaya might not be authentic New Orleans, but it was a feast for the senses. "I think it's perfect, Pa. Best you've ever made."

"Good." Milo snatched the spoon from her and stirred the huge pot of rice, tomatoes, chicken, broth and sausage. Pale green celery dotted the red and white. Next to the stove, piles of translucent shrimp shimmered in a heap on a bright green ceramic platter. "But it needs a touch more red pepper."

"Maybe," she agreed. "But don't make it too spicy, Pa."

Not looking at her, he sprinkled pepper flakes carefully over the simmering mixture. "The boy. Oliver."

"Oliver." Gabby nodded. She didn't know whether to hope that Joe and his son would ring the doorbell or hope they wouldn't.

Every time she thought of Joe, her tummy fluttered, her pulse raced and she felt—agitated.

All this internal turmoil must mean she'd be disappointed if they canceled.

Or maybe it meant she didn't want to face the knowing glint in Joe Carpenter's brown eyes again.

What did she want?

She sensed that it was crucial that she figure out for herself what she'd wanted for herself in returning to Bayou Bend.

She looked around the homey kitchen with its worn wood cabinets and old linoleum floor. Milo's banged-up copper-bottomed pots hung from stainless steel hooks fixed into ceiling beams. On the counter over the double sink, the deep pink buds of a Christmas cactus hinted of the promise of the season, a reminder that darkness would end in light.

Spicy scents of past and present mingled with memories in a mixture as rich as Milo's jambalaya, scents evoking joy and laughter and warmth from earlier years.

Like the cactus, happiness was a prickly-leaved plant waiting to bloom.

That was why she'd come home. To find that joy she'd lost, the joy she believed in her heart Milo needed.

What *did* she want?

And where did Joe Carpenter and his son fit into the new life she was shaping?

She wanted the best Christmas she could make, and being around Joe made her sparkle and feel alive. Made her look forward to the next hour or day, when she hadn't looked forward to anything since her mother's death.

Being around Joe made her feel like the Christmas cactus, all tight pink buds waiting to burst forth.

If he decided to take a pass on an impulsively issued invitation, she couldn't blame him.

But as her attention focused on the cactus buds, the truth slapped her in the face.

She wanted him and Oliver to ring her doorbell. She wanted them in this old house, sharing the tradition of arranging ornaments to hide the bare spots on the tree. She wanted to see them spoon out heaping bowls of jambalaya and hear them sing carols around the ancient upright piano.

She wanted all the corny, traditional trappings of the holiday, all the gaudy color and glitter and sound. She longed to surround herself with heaps of packages wrapped in shiny red-and-gold paper and elaborately tied bows.

For whatever reason, she wanted Joe and Oliver to be part of that richness, not left by themselves to celebrate Christmas in a hotel on the highway.

"Hope these damn shrimp taste as good as they look." Milo held a glistening shrimp up to the light and examined it critically before adding so casually that Gabrielle was immediately alerted, "Didn't know you know Joe Carpenter?"

She knew what he was doing. Joe Carpenter wasn't the real issue. Her dad wanted to talk. Like a cat stalking a bird, he'd sneak up on what he really wanted to talk about and, sooner or later, pounce.

That's when the feathers would fly.

She could wait.

Because Milo wasn't happy with her. She was pretty sure he was ready to launch into a lecture about her return to Bayou Bend, and she was in no hurry to tangle over this particular subject with a stubborn Irishman.

Double dose of hardheaded, is what she called him.

"So how do you happen to know Carpenter?" He plopped a shrimp back onto the heap.

"It's a small town, Pa. Why wouldn't I know him?"

"Bayou Bend's small, all right. Folks know everybody's business more than they should. Seems funny, though, you knowing Joe. He's older than you, and he left town before you were in high school."

"No, he left his senior year. I was in tenth grade. I used to see him around town. That's all." She wasn't about to tell her dad about that long-ago night. Harmless as it had been, it felt private. Special.

"That's right. You were only a sophomore. I'd forgotten." His frown disappeared. "So you saw him at Tibo's and invited him? That's all?"

Puzzled, Gabrielle glanced at her dad. "Sure. Why? Is inviting him a problem?"

"No." Milo poked at the shrimp, cleared his throat. "Just— oh, Joe Carpenter's had a hard life, least that's what I've heard. I wouldn't want you getting hurt, that's all."

Gabrielle avoided addressing the implied question. "It was a friendly invitation to new neighbors, nothing more. Is there a problem?"

"Nope. Not at all. Joe's welcome in my house."

"Maybe not in other houses?"

"Probably not in a lot of houses," Milo agreed.

Joe's tough, don't-give-a-damn exterior made it difficult to see him as vulnerable to the town's opinion, but her heart ached as she imagined Joe with his son, seeking shelter from Bayou Bend's coldness. He needed a friend.

She could be a friend.

"Here, Pa. Your scalpel." Gabrielle handed him the deveining knife. Poking her father lightly on the shoulder, she studied him surreptitiously.

Usually thin, he'd lost even more weight since she'd last visited.

"Thanks, honey." He ran the knife down the back spine of the shrimp, discarding the vein on a paper.

"Want help?"

"Nope."

Thinking of the conversation the day before at the tree lot, Gabrielle added, "Didn't know you'd had Joe Carpenter to dinner."

"Not recently." Milo pitched the shrimp into the colander,

picked up another. "And it wasn't exactly a dinner party, for your information, missy."

"You're making me curious, Pa."

"Well, we know what curiosity did to the cat."

Gabrielle opened the refrigerator and found the mushrooms and red onions she'd sliced earlier. Digging around the overloaded interior, she plucked out bags of lettuces and endive. "I can't help being interested."

"Be interested. That's fine." He ignored her whuff of exasperation.

"You're not going to tell me, are you?" Gabby tilted her head.

"Not my place to. If you're so interested, ask Joe. It's his business. If he wants you to know, he can tell you. I already told you Joe and his son were welcome here." Holding up the knife and using it as a pointer, he stopped her midsyllable. "And that's all I'm going to say about *that,* Gabrielle, so don't go poking around trying to make me tell you, hear?"

"We'll see." From under lowered lashes, she glanced at her dad.

He groaned. "I know what that means. You're going to pester me until you winkle out what you want to know, aren't you?"

"Probably. After all, I learned from the master. I didn't grow up a lawyer's daughter without picking up a few tricks."

He shook his head, grinning back at her. "My sins are coming back to haunt me. And speaking of coming back—"

Interrupting him, a tiger-striped cat thudded onto the counter.

"Down, Cletis!" Flapping her hand, Gabrielle made frantic shoo-shoo motions at him. "Take your greedy self off this counter this instant. If you know what's good for you."

Cocking a hind leg and licking it, Cletis mewed inquisitively, "Mrrrr?"

"Yes, you, mister. I mean it. Down. Now."

Working his head under a paper bag lying on the counter, he made himself as invisible as twenty pounds of fur-covered creature could.

"Sorry, buster, I can see you." Gabrielle hoisted the cat off the counter and took out a saucer from the cabinet.

His attempt to hide from her was no more successful than hers had been as she knelt at Joe Carpenter's well-shod feet yesterday. An errant sympathy for Cletis moved her to swipe a piece of sausage from the jambalaya.

Chopping up bits of sausage, she used her hip and leg to keep him on the floor even as he chirped and twined himself around her legs. "Here, beast." She placed the saucer on the floor and stooped to scratch him between the ears. "You are one spoiled fat boy."

Cletis slurped and gnawed enthusiastically.

Milo was suspiciously quiet.

Kneading the cat's head, Gabrielle glanced up at her dad. "You've been letting him on the counter, haven't you, Pa?"

"Once in a while."

Cletis nibbled her thumb as she started to stand up. "Hah. Every night is my guess." She could understand. The cat was company for her dad. "Lord, he's gained weight while you've lost at least ten pounds. You're feeding him and not making meals for yourself, just nibbling from the refrigerator and counter, not sitting down for a real dinner, right? It's a good thing I came home to take care of you."

Milo thwacked the spoon on the edge of the pot. "That's what I want to talk to you about, missy."

"And what's that?" Gabrielle rested her arms gently around her dad's bony shoulders. As she'd thought, the discussion about Joe was a red herring. Push had finally come to shove.

"This damn fool notion you have. That you have to look after me. What makes you think I need any help? I have most of my hair, my hearing and, with bifocals, I see pretty damn well." He slapped the spoon on the counter.

Cletis looked up hopefully.

"You're not taking care of yourself, Pa. I can see that. You look worse than when I came home when you were in the hospital. You haven't bounced back from your surgery."

"It was minor surgery, and Doc Padgett says I'm fine. I feel fine. So I'm fine, Gabrielle. This nonsense about selling your business and moving back to Bayou Bend is—" He frowned, twirled the spoon between his fingers. Rice grains speckled the counter. "Honey, I love you. You know that. And I'm pleased as punch you're home. For a while."

A sharp pang whipped through her. She went motionless, stunned by the unexpected pain and sense of rejection.

"Now, don't look at me like that." He patted her hand. "I'm doing fine. We should have talked over this decision of yours before you leaped headfirst into this kind of change."

Gabrielle decided to be as blunt as he had been. "Pa, I don't like the way you look. Your face has all the color of a banker's suit. I think you're sick—"

"Damn it, missy. I was in the hospital for three weeks before Thanksgiving. I lost my appetite, that's all." He scowled at her. "I was a skinny guy even before my surgery."

"And I wouldn't have known you were having surgery if Taylor Padgett hadn't called me."

"I'm right annoyed with that boy, too."

Taylor Padgett was thirty-six years old and had been practicing in Bayou Bend ever since he'd finished medical school. "Why?" she asked with exaggerated patience.

"I didn't want him bothering you."

"Bothering me? *Bothering* me?" Pacing in a circle, she waved her arms in frustration. "Heaven forbid that my aged father should *bother* me. I certainly wouldn't want to miss out on my busy social schedule because my *father* was in the *hospital*."

He picked up another shrimp and sliced it down the back. "You're worrying too much, Gabrielle. And I may be sixty-four years old, but I'm not *aged,* so don't get sassy." Head down, his fists balancing him on the counter, he stopped, sighed. "Somehow you got it in your head that I can't manage alone since your mama died."

"Pa, I didn't mean to upset you." Gabrielle rested her cheek against his paper-thin one. She remembered too well her panic at the sight of her strong, bullheaded dad surrounded by tubes and IVs. "I want you to get well, to be your old ornery self."

He snapped his head up and went back to deveining shrimp with a vengeance. "Then don't worry me any more with this idiotic plan of sacrificing your life to look after me, Gabrielle Marie. You're a good girl, and you mean well, but, honey, I'm fine. I don't need you here to baby-sit me."

Again that slice of pain. "Pa—"

He gestured her quiet. "Go back to Arizona after New Year's and get on with your life. I don't want you giving up your life because of some dopey idea that I'm headed into a decline."

"Dopey, Pa? Thanks a lot." His word made her laugh out loud. Her dad was trying too hard.

"Gabrielle Marie, I fully intend to live another twenty or thirty years, and I'm going to have myself one hell of a terrific old age. You're making a big fuss out of nothing. I'd tell you if I were ill. Trust me."

She didn't. And he wouldn't. He would try to protect her with his last breath, that's what Milo O'Shea would do. "I'm here, Pa. I'm staying."

Smelling of brine and cayenne, he hugged her tightly. "Not that I don't appreciate the offer, honey, but I'm not looking for a keeper. Not yet."

"Pa, it's too late. I sold the house-sitting agency. I sold my condo. Yes—" she forestalled his inevitable question "—I made money on both." She tapped his forehead, enumerating. "I gave away my plants. My aquarium. I'm home. You're not going to be alone anymore. I'll keep you company in the evening. I'm going to make you nutritious meals.''

Exasperation tightened his mouth into a line. "And I reckon you're going to keep Cletis off the counter.''

She nodded.

"Sounds like the seventh circle of hell.''

"I've made my decision. It's a done deal.''

"Hell's bells, Gabrielle. You really sold everything?'' His voice was dismayed.

She sat down abruptly, shaken by his insistence. Suddenly she wondered if she'd misread all the signs that had sent her to the Realty office. "Except the car.''

Her dad blew an explosive raspberry of annoyance, a sound she knew all too well. "Missy, didn't you hear a word I said?''

Standing up, she walked over to him. "I heard you, Pa.'' She kissed the top of his head. When had he shrunken so much that she could easily plant a kiss on that saucer-size bald spot? He did need her, no matter what he pretended. She'd done the right thing. For him.

For herself.

"Gabrielle, honey,'' her dad said slowly, patiently, "I'm not lonely. The old coots and I haven't given up our Saturday morning coffee at Bell's Diner. I'm not sitting around waiting for the Grim Reaper. I miss your mama, that will never change, but I'm making friends, going on field trips.'' He laughed. "Sixty-four years old and going on field trips for the first time in my life.''

"You gave up driving?'' She was truly worried now. Milo would never give up driving. Driving was in his blood. He loved cars.

"Lord, honey, I still drive. I got talked into these overnight field trips around the state, and I kind of like them. Interesting folks going to interesting places. People I wouldn't have met if I hadn't stepped out and taken a chance on this program.''

"I don't understand what you're talking about. A program?"

"Oh…" His voice was lawyer-smooth and Gabrielle's antennae rose. "One of the hospital candy stripers told me about these outings the park district arranged."

Gabrielle was mystified. Milo was up to something, the fox. She'd find out—when Milo was ready for her to. "You go on field trips to tourist attractions?"

"Sure. Up to Tampa. To Atlanta. To shop."

"You go *shopping?* You hate shopping."

"Thought I did, honey, but life has a funny way of springing surprises on you. At the very moment you think you have everything figured out and you have a clear vision of what the rest of your life will be, well, darn if life doesn't pitch a high, hard fast ball your way. I've had calm and serene for most of my life. I'm ready for wild and woolly. Anyway, who said you can't teach an old dog new tricks?" Throwing his head back, he laughed, and the sound was so natural and warm that she would have believed him if she couldn't see his gray skin and fatigue.

"Sure, Pa." She wondered why shopping seemed like a wild-and-woolly adventure, but if it worked for him, that was good enough for her. "Whatever you say. But you're still stuck with me."

"We'll see, missy. We'll see." Something in his chuckle made her lift her head and stare at him.

The clanging of the old-style bell ringer startled them both. They gaped at each other, then at the clock.

"Good grief, where did the time go?" Gabrielle's heart did double-time, and her cheeks flushed hot. *Joe.*

"I see we can't cook and have a serious conversation at the same time. Now *that,* honey, *is* a sign of old age." He scraped the pile of garbage off the counter and into the trash. "Get the door. I have to wash up." Moving rapidly, he poured lemon juice over his hands and then stuck them under the faucet.

Gabrielle blinked. What on earth? Her dad's mottled cheeks were as pink as hers felt. The gray she'd seen earlier had vanished with the rush of blood to his face. "You okay?"

She wasn't about to walk out of the room and leave him to have a heart attack on the floor.

"What?" Distracted, he glanced at her over his shoulder and continued scrubbing his hands. Drying them, he checked his appearance in the miniature mirror next to the fridge. "I look okay?" He flattened his hair with still-damp hands.

"Sure, Pa." Gabrielle had never seen her father flustered like this. He must be too tired. Having a bunch of people over for a meal was apparently a bigger drain on his energy than either one of them had figured. She shouldn't have let him—

"Uh, Gabrielle." He hesitated. The deep breath he took left his belted pants sliding toward his hips. "There's something you and I need to discuss."

"Yes, Pa?" She spoke in a pleasant monotone designed to soothe him. He was upset. She didn't want to upset him any more.

He frowned. "Why are you talking so funny, missy? Like I've gone deaf or crazy." Before she could answer, he was scanning his appearance in the mirror again.

The doorbell clanged, a prolonged, raucous shriek.

"Go, go. Somebody's here. Get the door. Don't want to keep anyone waiting."

Strolling to the door, Gabrielle sorted out her impressions. Without a question, her dad was up to something.

She opened the door to cool darkness and Joe Carpenter leaning against her doorjamb. Her heart stuttered and galloped as he smiled at her. Oh, yes, all that heart-thumping and face-flushing meant she wanted to see Joe Carpenter again.

Wary and on the verge of a frown, Oliver stepped out from

LINDSAY LONGFORD 51

behind the safety of his dad. The cowlick was nowhere in existence. Joe must have smashed Oliver's hair down with industrial-strength hair control.

She wanted to hug them both. Oliver, because the boy needed hugging. Joe? Well, just because. Her mouth curved in sudden happiness, everything inside her blazing with expectation and—*lightness.*

She felt as if a skyful of stars had taken residence inside her tummy, burning and tumbling and glowing.

The screen door squeaked as she swung it wider. "Hi, guys. Come on in. Hungry?"

Clutching a mangled paper cone of flowers, Oliver plopped one foot over her threshold, hesitated, turned toward Joe, who nudged him forward.

"Here." Oliver thrust the flowers at her. "Hostess gift."

"Thank you very much." Taking the offering, Gabrielle sniffed at the roses and white orchids surrounded by long-needled pine and baby's breath. Cold and sweet, their faint fragrance floated to her. "They're beautiful, Oliver."

Freed of the flowers, he grabbed Joe's hand. "I didn't pick 'em out."

"That's all right. It's the thought that counts."

The look that crossed their faces at the same time could only be described as desperate. They looked equally uncomfortable.

"We weren't sure what to bring." Joe raised his hand as if he were going to touch her, as if he didn't quite know whether to shake her hand or—

Gabrielle motioned them in, the thought of the *or* sending another wave of flame through her. "Pa's in the kitchen finishing up the jambalaya."

Behind her a pot lid clattered to the floor.

"Damn, Cletis. Now look what you've done!"

"Milo making a guest feel at home?" Joe's eyebrow angled skyward in amusement.

"Whoops!" Gabrielle pulled at Joe's arm and slammed the screen door behind him.

A weight of fur collapsed onto her feet and rolled off, panting.

Looking down at the cat lying belly-up in front of him, Joe drawled, "Cletis, I take it?"

The cat's legs sprawled in abandon, his belly flattening against the floor like a pancake.

"He's an insider kitty, but he has a yen for the forbidden, so we have to watch him. He's faster than he looks, but that's not saying much."

"A cat! I like cats." Oliver dropped to his knees. "Can I touch him?"

"Sure. He won't bite. Or scratch. Takes too much energy. He just wants to be worshiped and adored." In an aside, she murmured sweetly to Joe, "Like most guys."

"Cruel." Joe flicked her chin. "Whatever happened to peace on earth and good will to men?"

"Oh, golly, men don't like to be adored?"

"Of course we do. Nothin' like a pretty woman making goo-goo eyes to make us feel all manly and studly, ma'am." His drawl was pure provocation as he tipped an imaginary cowboy hat in her direction.

Cradling the flowers, she laughed at him, her heart thumping like crazy. "I don't think you ever needed anyone's goo-goo eyes, Carpenter, to make you feel studly."

"Ah, you noticed, huh?"

She motioned for him to follow her to the kitchen. "Didn't everyone?"

"Good to know all that effort wasn't wasted. You going to stay with the cat, Oliver, or come with us?"

With his chin resting against Cletis's neck, Oliver considered them, hesitated, then finally decided as Cletis batted a paw against his face. "Maybe I'll stay with him so he has company. He wants me to."

"Looks that way to me." Joe stooped and rubbed his knuckles along the cat's belly.

Watching his long, lean fingers work into the fur of the cat's stomach, Gabrielle swallowed. Like Cletis, she felt the urge to purr.

Instead, she bent to Oliver and directed his attention to the chest near the door. "If you open this drawer, you'll find some kitty treats. We keep them here so we have a better chance of luring him back inside if he goes for a walk on the wild side."

"Okay." Oliver grabbed a treat and held it in his palm, waiting for Cletis to roll upright.

Cletis, however, merely turned his head, watching expectantly until Oliver held the mouse-shaped munchy close enough so that the cat only had to stick out a rough tongue and lap Oliver's hand.

"Another guy habit?" Leaning in close to her, Joe murmured in her ear, and his breath eased its way inside her, into her lungs, her blood.

"Probably."

"Think I'll go through my next life as a Cletis clone, then." Joe stood up, holding a hand to her. "Wait for the munchies to come your way. No hunting, no effort. He has the right idea."

The glance he shot her way made her decide that the kind of munchies Joe meant didn't come prepackaged. She rose at the same time and her hip bumped his, his hand slid along her side, and her whole body went soft and boneless. Her breath hitched in her throat, and she wanted to say something clever, something to lighten that terrible awareness, to make it unimportant.

She couldn't let it be important.

Oliver chortled, "Tickles!" as Cletis scoured his face with a lazy tongue. Joe turned to his son, and Gabrielle's lungs expanded, inhaled, releasing her.

"The kitchen's this way." Her breathing shallow, Gabrielle

brushed her hair away from her blazing cheeks and hurried toward the sound of slamming pots and rushing water.

"Going to put me to work?" Leading her forward, Joe rested his hand at the waist of her dress.

"Of course. The devil makes work for idle hands."

"Too easy, Gabby," he murmured, and the creases around his eyes deepened with laughter, the brown turning almost golden as he turned his head.

"I'll let that one pass."

Under the pressure of his fingers, the brushed rayon fabric of her dress slithered under his palm as she moved, stroked against her skin. The touch of cool, slick material over her body and the press of his warm hand created an unbearable tension in her. She wanted to lean back against his hand, move against it. Her belly, her breasts, *everything* ached, tightened as he flexed his hand.

A simple touch. A polite gesture.

Nothing more.

But his palm might as well have been flat against her naked skin, and politeness and good manners had nothing at all to do with the spritz and sizzle inside her.

Gabrielle quickly stepped ahead of him, and under her thin dress, the curve of her waist where he'd touched her felt chilled as his hand fell away. Oddly bereft.

She shivered.

She'd liked the touch of his hand on her.

She might be as essentially inexperienced as that girl she'd been when he first kissed her, but she was old enough to know what was happening to her body.

No wonder she'd resisted making love, having sex.

All these years of dating and kissing, and she'd had no idea of the power of need. Of desire.

In the most essential way, Joe Carpenter had imprinted that adolescent girl she'd been with the scent and feel of him, imprinted her for life.

No wonder she'd never found anyone who made her feel as if her very breath were his, his heartbeat hers.

Like a chick imprinted, her body followed Joe, obeying some primitive, brain-deep command of scent and touch, some primal command over which she had no control.

She was in trouble.

Because, no matter how she figured the numbers, Joe Carpenter and Gabrielle O'Shea didn't add up in anybody's math equation.

Chapter Four

"Gabrielle, who's at the door?" A dish towel tucked into the waistband of his navy slacks, Milo came into the hall. His gaze passed over Joe, focused on the front door, returned to Gabby.

"Joe and Oliver."

"Oh?" Slightly formal, a bit distant, Milo's question sent Joe's heart rate into second gear. "I don't see the boy."

"Oliver's still in the front hall. With Cletis." Pausing in the bough-and-ribbon-draped alcove between dining room and living room, she looked over her shoulder.

Her smile came slowly, gently, all tipped corners and softness, a miracle of its own slowing his pulse to molasses. Joe didn't understand the reassurance in her greeny-brown eyes, but he welcomed it, luxuriated in the warmth of that smile that sneaked through the chill icing his heart.

With that smile, she made him feel as if he had an ally. She'd smiled at him the same way she had that day he'd first seen her outside Forester's Fresh Foods.

This time she wasn't thirteen, though.

This time he was smart enough to know what a gift a smile like that was.

And, seeing Milo O'Shea again, Joe conceded he liked having Milo's daughter in his corner.

For a moment he wondered what Milo intended—wondered, too, what Milo had told Gabby. Joe tightened his mouth, preparing for anything that might happen. If Milo had told Gabby about that night long ago when Joe had run from Bayou Bend, would she still look at him with eyes wide and dark with flirtation? Or would her eyes hold the contempt he'd sensed in everyone else's eyes all those years ago even before that last night?

He didn't think Milo would have said anything to her, but Milo held all the cards. Joe was on Milo's turf. Whatever was said, not said, was Milo's decision.

Looking back down the hall toward his son, Joe hated the sense of helplessness that washed through him.

He liked being in control of his life, and nothing except the decision to return to Bayou Bend had been in his control since he'd gone to find the boy.

The boy who *might* be his son.

Or *might not* be.

There were questions there, too, questions he'd have to decide how to handle. For himself. For Oliver.

Tricky, that little question.

He'd chosen to return to Bayou Bend because he thought it offered a stable, safe environment for a child who'd never had either. This town could be good for Oliver. While folks didn't leave their doors unlocked at night anymore, even here, Bayou Bend offered the benefits of small-town life, a place where Oliver could ride his bicycle down the sidewalk, and Joe wouldn't have nightmares about drug pushers and kidnappers. In this town, if everything worked out, Oliver would be safe.

Truth to tell, Joe thought as Milo's gaze fixed on him,

Bayou Bend was the only place he had any attachment to. And maybe a negative attachment was better than nothing.

At seventeen, with a chip on his shoulder, maybe he wouldn't have liked any place his old man had dragged him to. At least in Bayou Bend, he was familiar with what would be expected of him as he tried to make a family for Oliver and him.

And if Joe Carpenter was the last person anyone in the town would have expected to come back as a sedate family man, the town could take its opinions and—

Midthought, Joe stopped.

Places changed. People changed.

He had to give the town a chance if he expected it to return the favor. He'd strolled down its streets with that chip on his shoulder once before. That attitude had brought him nothing but trouble and a fast ticket out of town.

He would do whatever he had to, to make this work.

He just hoped he hadn't made a mistake.

Narrowing his eyes, he met Milo's gaze straight on. What would be, would be.

"Joe." Milo stuck out a wide-palmed hand and grasped Joe's. "Good to see you, son."

"You, too." Joe nodded. He ignored the lump in his throat. Milo had called him *son*. He was going to make the situation easy for Oliver. For Joe.

They'd taken the first hurdle.

"I hear you make a killer jambalaya, Milo. Thanks for including us."

"The more the merrier."

Gabby's laugh was a silvery chime that slipped along Joe's skin, tightening it. "Moon told Joe you'd say that."

"Did he, now?" Milo shrugged.

Joe wondered if he'd been mistaken. Was he going to have to collect his son and bolt for the door after all? "Not that it matters," he said evenly, "but it was Moon who actually invited us to your party."

"Son of a gun." Milo laughed. "That boy's a friendly cuss, even with somebody else's hospitality."

"Pa, *I* invited Joe and Oliver, too." Facing her dad, posture rigid, head up, Gabby reminded Joe of a kitten facing off with the head tomcat. All she needed was claws and a good loud hiss. Once again, her defense of him eased a tightness in his chest, warmed him in the glow of her kindness.

"Shoot, honey, you already told me that. Joe's welcome, and so's his boy, no matter *who* invited them. Don't go getting your hackles up, hear me?"

Not sure who Milo was directing that final comment to, Joe felt his own hackles lie right back down and relief flow through his tensed muscles. He hadn't realized until that moment how keyed up he'd been about this encounter.

Milo was cool about the situation.

He'd welcomed Joe.

But as he shook hands with the man who had changed his life, Joe wondered how Milo would have reacted if he'd seen Joe about to plant a kiss on Milo's darling daughter at Moon's yesterday.

Knowing that, would Milo have been quite so cool about having Joe Carpenter in his home?

Not likely.

One more reason to keep his distance from Gabby.

Too much at stake.

"Come on into the kitchen, Joe. Everybody hangs out there."

"Don't know what we need a living room for, Gabrielle. Nobody uses it," Milo grumbled. "We'll find a job for you, Joe. Let you get messy with the rest of us."

"Fine."

The ringer on the door clamored for attention, and Milo did

a brisk about-face. "I'll see who this is. You all go on. Gabby, take care of Joe. Set him to work, hear?"

"I hear you, Pa." Gabby half turned to look at Milo as he scurried toward the front door. "It's probably Moon."

"Could be." Not stopping, Milo called back, "Or it might be some of my friends from the bus trips."

The concern that flashed over Gabby's face before she shuttered it with politeness caught Joe's attention and puzzled him. As she turned to him, her red-banded hem slithering over his slacks, he filed away the memory of her expression. He'd think about it another time. Later, when she wasn't right in front of him, distracting him with her voice, her *self*.

"I told you we'd make you sing for your supper, didn't I?"

Resisting the urge to take two fingers and smooth away the line between her eyebrows, he stuck a hand in his pocket. "In fact, what you said was that you'd put Oliver and me to work. Singing's an entirely different matter."

"We might make you sing. Later."

"Don't want to go there." He leaned against the wall. "You've never heard me sing."

"Can't sing, poor baby?"

"I can sing." Joe liked the way her clingy gold dress with the red bands at the bottom and around the sleeves burnished her skin with reflected gold.

She shimmered in front of him, her dress shifting, shining, slipping over her hipbones, drawing his attention with her every move. Like the red bands on her dress, her cheeks bloomed with color as she teased him. "If you can sing, what's the problem?"

"I sing like a frog with indigestion."

She sputtered with laughter. "I see. In that case, you're safe." She turned to push open the kitchen door. "Umm, Joe?"

"Yes, Gabby?" He hesitated. One step more would bring

him so close to her that her elusive fragrance would wrap around him once more.

A smart man wouldn't take that step. He pushed himself free of the wall, anticipation thrumming inside him.

A man who had a child dependent on him absolutely would not take that single, dangerous step closer to Gabby and her gold dress.

He relaxed against the wall again. "You had a question, sweet pea?"

"What *does* a frog in gastric distress sound like?"

Following Gabby past the alcove and into the kitchen, Joe reminded himself one more time that he couldn't let himself slip again the way he had yesterday. He'd have to keep his guard up around her.

For a man like him, Gabrielle should erect a Keep Away sign that was billboard high and neon bright.

He wished he could understand his yearning for her. Not exactly lust, something different, something *more*. His need to be around her distracted him. Yielding to distraction could destroy everything if he didn't watch himself.

But damned if the little distraction herself didn't walk right up to him, put her arms around his waist. Her hands moved, flattened, turned against him.

Her light scent was a teasing sweetness in his brain, and he wanted to bend closer to her, breathe more deeply of that sweetness that flowed through him and sang in his blood. Where had this need come from, this need to breathe her essence, this need to taste her?

He tipped his head.

She stepped back with satisfaction. "There, Joe."

"What?"

Hands on her hips, she surveyed him, mischief lighting up her eyes. "Don't want you getting shrimp juice and tomato sauce on your elegant slacks."

Joe glanced down. Like Milo, he now wore a dishcloth

apron around his waist. She'd tucked the cloth neatly into his belt loops and waistband so quickly he hadn't even realized what she was up to. Taking a breath, he pitched his voice so low that only she could hear. "You're a sly boots, Gabby O'Shea, aren't you?"

"Me?" Reaching behind her, she removed a red apron from a hook on the wall. Festooned with silver bells and painted packages, the apron swallowed her. Its bells jingled as she moved with rapid, dancelike steps to the massive round table in the middle of the kitchen. "Nah. I'm only being thoughtful. A good hostess takes care of her guests," she said primly, flicking a bell out of the way as she tied the wide sash around her waist.

"I'll keep that in mind." He reached out and set one of the bells to jingling. "In case I need any—care."

Her face flushed, and she looked away from him, frowning.

His frown came on the shadow of hers. He cleared his throat. Looking for a task, he picked up a platter of plastic-covered hors d'oeuvres. Shifted it from hand to hand. Put it back down.

Flirting with Gabby was stupid.

It was the season, that was all.

A pretty woman, carols in the air and the warmth of this house seeped into him and made him feel as if he belonged—somewhere.

And flirting with Gabby was so easy, so pleasurable, so *right*.

Returning to Bayou Bend was bringing back too many of his bad habits. He *liked* women. This thing with Gabby, though, this went beyond his experience. *Liking* he understood. He didn't understand this mix of emotions he was experiencing around her, this amalgam of past and present, of Christmas and loneliness and hope all linking together and making him *want*.

Silently he went to work on the salad she pointed out to

him, and as streams of people threaded in and out of the kitchen, Joe watched her, saw her easy teasing of the guests, watched her fetch and carry glasses of wine, watched her kiss Moon, who dangled a sprig of mistletoe over her head and demanded a kiss.

She made it all seem effortless, all the work and bustle fueling her until the air around her seemed to shine with the gold of her dress.

He couldn't take his eyes off the shine and glitter that was Gabby O'Shea.

Gradually the kitchen emptied as she directed people to the boxes of ornaments. "Pick one and hang it on the tree, Taylor," she said to the man she'd introduced as Milo's doctor. "Moon, you have to do the lights because you're the tallest."

Grumbling and laughing, they followed her directions until Joe was the only one left.

"Heads up." Gabby's bells alerted him, and he ducked as she passed him with a platter.

"That phrase has never made sense to me. It's guaranteed to make you look up."

"It's one of those warnings we ignore in spite of good sense, I suppose." She stuffed a shrimp in his mouth and jingled away in a swirl of red and gold. The kitchen door swung shut behind her.

"Damn right," he muttered through a mouthful of spicy shrimp. "Any fool with an ounce of brains would know better than to stick his head in harms's way." He chewed slowly. "And yet we keep sticking our heads up. Serves us right when we get beaned."

The kitchen door slammed open against the wall. Gabby danced by him, a whirl of bells and bright red fabric. "Sorry. I didn't hear you, Joe. What did you say?"

"Nothing important. A reminder to myself, that's all." He leaned against the counter. How could this slip of a girl, this *woman*, make him ignore all the warnings of his own brain?

"Give me another job, Gabby." Even with the warning still echoing in his brain, he extended his arms slowly, bracketing her waist between them. The heat of her body warmed his wrists. The shape of her enticed him as if he could feel her beneath his hands. His palms curved the air between them.

He didn't touch her.

"Right. Those idle hands the devil's looking for." Breathy, her voice rubbed against his nerve endings. Her gaze dropped to the floor and she stepped back, away from him. Her face matched her apron as she grabbed a wooden spoon from a poinsettia-shaped ceramic dish near the stove. Handle first, she handed the spoon to him. Rice grains dripped to the floor. "How are you at stirring?" Still not looking at him, she stooped to scrape up the rice.

"I've been accused of stirring up trouble a few times."

Standing slowly, she said softly, so softly that he had to lean forward to hear her, "Is that what you're doing now, Joe? Stirring up trouble?"

He rotated the spoon between his fingers, studying its spinning bowl, which held no answers, before he finally sighed and said, "I don't know, Gabby. Maybe flirting with you a little."

"Flirting's as natural to you as breathing. This—" her hand fluttered in front of him "—seems different. I don't know how—" she stopped, continued "—to react. You make me feel—"

Again she stopped, and he stared into her troubled face, stung by the uneasiness he sensed in her.

"How do I make you feel, Gabby?"

She straightened her shoulders, looked around the kitchen as the words rushed out so fast he figured she hadn't meant to say them. "Female. Fluttery. And I don't know whether I like feeling this way."

His unreliable conscience, long dormant, struggled to the surface and made him offer. "Do you want me to leave,

Gabby? I will.'' He placed the spoon carefully on the counter behind him.

Not answering, she looked everywhere except at him.

He smelled the spicy richness of the jambalaya, heard the muffled sounds of laughter from the hall and living room, felt the weight of the air in the room heavy on his skin, and waited, feeling oddly like a man about to be sentenced. Until he'd offered to leave, he hadn't known how much he wanted to stay. ''Say the word. I'll go.''

On a long exhalation, she said, ''Stay.'' The word hovered between them.

''Why?'' he asked baldly, everything in him poised to leave this place that felt like a sanctuary.

''I want you to.''

''Why?''

Her words came slowly, measured out as if with an eye-dropper. ''I don't know.''

His lungs expanded, filled with air. He hadn't realized he'd been holding his breath until that moment. He felt light-headed, dizzy. ''I'm making you uncomfortable.''

''Oh, yes.'' She nodded hard, the bells on her apron jingling, and one strand of hair flipping against her cheek. ''You do.''

He lifted the strand up, twined it around his finger and tucked it behind her ear. ''I kind of like knowing I make you—fluttery. But I don't mean to make you uncomfortable, Gabrielle Marie.''

Her laugh burbled up, shakily, her breath fluttering against his hand as it stilled in front of her face. ''Joe Carpenter, I don't think you could help making me uncomfortable, no matter how hard you tried.''

He didn't pretend not to know what she meant. Meeting her honesty with his own, he said, ''There's something going on between us, isn't there? Some electricity neither of us wants?''

She dipped her chin, hesitated. ''There's something, yes.''

Lifting her chin, she waited for a moment while his heart drummed heavily inside him. "I'm not good at flirting, Joe." She stuck her hands into the pockets of her apron and tiny bells chimed. "You are."

He didn't miss that she'd skirted his second question. "I like women, Gabby. I like to tease, to flirt."

"I know." Something he didn't quite understand shivered underneath her admission.

"Flirting doesn't mean anything." Trying to keep the mood light because that inexplicable note he'd heard in her voice disturbed him, he shot her a shuck-and-jive grin. The words felt like a lie. The attitude had begun to feel like a lie for a long time now, and being around Gabby made it worse. But he thought he could defuse the intensity and turn the situation into something casual that would relieve her anxiety. "Flirting's not important. No harm in it. It's only playing around, that's all."

"I know."

He tapped her chin, the supple skin creamy soft beneath his touch. "Gettin' in a rut, Gabby. You're repeating yourself, sweet pea."

"I—" She laughed, and the shadow he'd seen moments ago in her eyes vanished with the laughter. "I almost said it again, didn't I?"

"Almost."

"Party nerves."

"Think so?" Because she'd retreated further than he intended, contrariness seized him, and he wanted to push her, to break through this brittleness and make her admit— What? That she liked the sizzle between them? Was that what he wanted from her? That admission she'd avoided earlier? "Sure it's not that...*something* popping between us?"

"Joe," she said, holding her hands out to him, palm up, warding him off, or warning him away, he wasn't altogether sure, "you can't help flirting any more than you can stop yourself from breathing. I'm not in your league. You need to play with someone who's up to your speed."

"Suppose I want to play with you, Gabby? What then?" He didn't want her to retreat into polite distance. He wanted her to look at him again as if she were on his side, in his corner. As if he were special to her.

Abruptly, she turned away from him, and the column of thin gold fabric showing in the gap at the back of her red apron was like a golden flame drawing him nearer, to see if its heat was real.

He remained slouched against the counter. Fire burned.

When she turned back to face him, her eyes were guarded, her face pale. "Joe, I like being around you. I like *you*. I like Oliver."

"He's a tough little nut. Sometimes he's not easy to like. And I'm not, either. Truth to tell, Gabby, I'm not an easy man."

"No, you're not." At the base of her neck, her skin flushed. "And if we're into truth telling, yes, that *something* between us makes me nervous. Because I'm not good at games, not the kind you're talking about playing, anyway." Her smile wavered, but she plunged on, and he was touched by her courage. "You throw me off balance." She looked up at him, her eyes dark, the tiny flame of himself in their center. "I don't know what the rules are. That's all." Her hands fell to her sides. "I don't know what you expect from me. In your game."

"Nothing. That's what, Gabby. And there aren't any rules." He wanted to touch her, he wanted to comfort her, he wanted to ease his mouth over hers and drink from the well of her sweetness. He took another step closer, trying to make sense for himself, for her, of the confusion roiling inside him. "I came back to this town because of my son. I have to figure out the best way to give him the kind of life I didn't have."

"Yes, you do. He needs you." Her attention was intent upon him.

"I know how to play the male-female game, Gabby. I don't know how to play the daddy game. In my own way, I'm struggling to sort out what's going on in my life, and you were there at Tibo's, all shiny and sparkly, and I wanted to spend a little time with you. I like being around you." He ran a hand through his hair, trying to explain the need he had to hear her laugh, the need to see her, to be near her. He shrugged, giving up. He didn't have the right words. He bent his knees so that he could look her straight in the eyes. "I don't want to hurt you, that's all I know."

"Are you afraid I'll expect something from you, Joe? Is that what you're trying to tell me?"

"We're real different, you and me, Gabby. I've always been an outsider in this town, and you're not. You'd have a right to expect—" He frowned as a smile blazed across her face.

Her attention sharpened as if a thought had occurred to her. "You're trying to be noble, aren't you? You're worried that I might misinterpret flirting as something else." She gave a strangled laugh. "You only want to *play* with me."

In spite of himself, he grinned, "Well, sweet pea, when you put it that way, it sounds kind of rascally, doesn't it?"

"But you *are* a rascal, Joe." She reached around him and retrieved the spoon he'd put down earlier. Handing it to him, she said, "Here. Stir the jambalaya so the rice doesn't stick. Add some of that chicken broth from the jar if you need to. Or the tomato juice. Either one's fine."

Not taking his eyes from hers, he stuck the spoon into the pot. "Uh, what's going on? I think you changed directions on me."

"Did I?" Her apron jingled merrily as she moved to the kitchen table for a platter. As if she'd reached a decision, her face was serene, the confusion gone.

"Yeah."

With the platter balanced in her hands, she said, "Everything's clear to me now. I needed the ground rules clarified, that's all. If you flirt with me, it's only a game. If I flirt with you, you're not going to expect anything from me." Shallow lines made dimple creases in her cheeks. "Like sex, for instance."

"Sex?" The heat that rioted through him right down to his groin had nothing to do with the word and everything to do with the prim purse of her mouth as she said it. If he kissed her, her mouth would purse up in that same way. At least with the first touch— "Sex?" he repeated, staggered by the thoughts rioting through his brain.

"Sure, sex. I only wanted to have everything out in the open. Cards on the table. No misunderstandings. You know." Her smile blazed like a comet through the air as she flipped past him. "So now we can flirt to our hearts' content."

Sex? Sex? Joe scrambled to clarify his overheated thoughts. Since she'd mentioned sex, he couldn't think of anything except the cling of her dress along her back, the clean line of her calves under the red hem of that slinky fabric. "Whoa, sweet pea. Who said anything about sex? Who asked? Who offered?"

Once more she danced through the kitchen door, letting it swing shut behind her.

"I'll be damned." Bits of sausage fell from his spoon back into the pot.

"Probably." Milo ambled through the door.

"Don't be rude, Milo." Beside him, a stunning, trim woman who looked to be close to Milo's age placed her hand in the crook of Milo's arm.

Clipping their heels, Gabby sailed back into view, red apron sails flapping at her side. Joe wondered if she saw the easy press of Milo's hand against the woman's arm.

"Meet Nettie Drew, Joe." Under Milo's bushy eyebrows,

his faded blue eyes brightened as his gaze returned to the woman.

"Hello." The hand Nettie extended was cool, lightly dotted with age spots. "I've already met your son. He and Cletis are currently under the tent of the dining room table. Occasionally they venture out for—" She looked up at Milo. "What did Oliver call it? Fodder?"

Milo nodded.

"That's an unusual word for a child his age. I was terribly impressed. He explained to me that it was a game he played with you. Weird words, he called it. We talked for quite a while before he retreated to the tent. He said he was observing feet."

"Is he making a pest of himself?" Sticking the spoon back on the poinsettia spoon rest, Joe prepared to go rescue Milo's guests from Oliver. And Cletis.

"Not at all. He's a charming boy." Nettie opened a drawer across from the table and took out a large serving spoon. "You should be proud of him."

"I am." Joe felt more than saw Gabby's movement toward his side. Again that sly warmth crept through him. A protective creature, she had a loyalty that wouldn't vanish like spit in the wind. But, sex? Gabby thinking about sex with him? Heat shot through him, a searing column of flame.

Nettie patted him on the arm. "Clearly you're a good father. The boy adores you."

Joe tried not to look at Milo. Milo would know better than anyone how unfit Joe was to be a parent. Milo would know what a joke it was, that Joe Carpenter could pretend to be a father, a responsible citizen of Bayou Bend.

"Got what you need, Nettie?" Milo draped his arm lightly around the woman's shoulders.

"Yes." The private smile she gave him would have gone unnoticed, but Joe saw Gabby turn at that exact moment, saw her go stick-stiff as Milo's hand slid over the curve of Nettie's hip.

"We can eat in a few minutes." Enveloped in her gaudy apron, Gabby looked forlorn as she observed her father. "We can finish decorating while we have supper. There's plenty of glogg still out on the buffet. Do you want some, Joe?"

Joe had had one cup of the hot Swedish drink with its combination of whisky, grain alcohol and brandy. And raisins. One was enough if he wanted to be able to walk straight for the rest of the night. "No, thanks."

"Pa? Nettie?" Brittleness turned her voice tight.

"No more for me, honey."

"I've had my limit, but thank you, Gabrielle. Milo told me it's Mary Kathleen's recipe that she made every year?" Nettie Drew's face was warmly sympathetic.

"Yes."

"How lovely that you would make it this year. You must have beautiful memories of her."

"Yes."

Joe couldn't stand the way Gabby's brightness dimmed with each second Nettie talked. "I need some help over here, sweet pea." He motioned to the pot. With his other hand, he waved Milo and Nettie out of the kitchen. "Go ahead. Gabby can show me what to do."

In the silence after Milo and Nettie left, Joe stirred and waited for Gabby to speak.

The bewilderment in her face touched him. The spark that usually lit her from the inside had vanished as if someone had blown out the candle. She looked pale and terribly fragile. He managed to resist the wayward impulse to gather her into his arms.

"You saw? Pa and Nettie?"

"Yeah." Giving her time to collect herself, he dug at the bottom of the pot, scraping loose the sticking rice. "Tough, huh?"

She nodded, a jerky wobble of her head. "I don't understand. Pa never told me." She slid along the wall into a sitting position. "This is…a surprise."

"You didn't know he was seeing anyone?"

"Oh." Stricken, she stared up at him. "You think it's serious?"

Joe turned off the burner and went to stoop beside her. Taking one of her hands, he unclenched the tight fist. "Yes, sweet pea, I think your dad is very serious about this woman. And I think she's crazy about him. In a very ladylike way, of course—subtle, nothing pushy or overt. She'd be a stunner at any age, and she's a very nice lady."

Gabby gulped. "Yes. You're right. She's nice."

"But?"

"She's not mama."

"Ah." Joe cupped her shoulder with his hands and rocked her back and forth gently. "You're jealous?"

She swiped her eyes with an abrupt movement, and he thought he saw a glint of moisture. "Jealous? You think I'd be so selfish I wouldn't want Pa to have a friend? You think I would begrudge him any comfort he could find?" She pushed Joe's hands away and struggled to her feet. "I'd be ashamed to behave like that."

"If you're not jealous, why are you so shaken, Gabby? Your dad's in his sixties. These days that's not so old. Why do you look like your world's caved in on top of you?"

Crossing her arms around herself, she stayed still for a long moment before saying, "I came back home because I thought Pa needed me. I wanted to believe that. I wanted it to be true. I told myself he was lonely." Her laugh was ragged. "I thought he was ill. And hiding the truth from me." A hiccuping sob rose from her throat.

"And now you don't know whether it was his need or your own that made your decision."

Her face crumpled, but she didn't cry. "I had a business,

friends, a place to live, but I wanted to come home, to be with Pa. I guess I misread the signs.''

"Because you wanted to."

"Because I wanted to." Turning her back to him, she laid her forehead against the wall. "Because I needed to."

Joe slipped his arm around her waist and turned her toward him. Pushing her head to his chest, he said, "We all look for someone to need us. Being needed, having someone to worry over, having someone to worry about us when we don't show up—that's one of the most basic human needs. Why should you be any different?''

Lying still in his arms, all her bright sassiness muted, she seemed infinitely vulnerable, and he wanted to shield her. He knew he couldn't. Gabby would have to come to terms with her decision and figure out for herself where she fit into her father's life now. What her own life would be.

Joe tightened his hold. Like Gabby, he couldn't see the terrifying future clearly. Like her, he would have to chart a new course for his life. Made with the best intentions, his decision to return to Bayou Bend, like hers, had far-reaching consequences.

Standing in the corner of her dad's kitchen with Joe Carpenter holding her as if she were a priceless vase, Gabrielle clung to him, her lifeline to safety on a rough sea.

Against her cheek, the steady, reassuring thump of Joe's heart anchored her.

Chapter Five

Gabrielle moved her hot cheek slowly against the cool, slick finish of Joe's shirt. She breathed in the clean, starchy fragrance, breathed in the clean smell of *him*. Joe Carpenter, offering her comfort in a dark moment.

The thump of his heart steadied her. He could make her feel dithery and fluttery and totally unlike herself. Now, with her heart aching, his touch calmed her and gave her a chance to pull herself together. Odd that it should be Joe Carpenter who had the power to soothe this pain inside her.

She had no tears, only this dislocation yawning like a chasm inside. Joe's touch was a bridge for her, a way back over the emptiness that opened beneath her. Clutching her fingers against his cotton shirt, she thanked heaven that he was there. Too hard to pretend in front of her dad and his Nettie. Too hard to hide all the hurt that rolled up like a tidal wave and crashed over her as she saw him with Nettie, the two of them with her on the outside.

"You okay?" Joe's hand cupped her nape, warm and comforting.

"I'm fine." She allowed herself the luxury of remaining within the circle of his arms, protected and safe. *Safe.* The word struck her as unexpected in the context of what she knew about Joe Carpenter. Or at least what she believed she knew about him. "No big deal. I overreacted, that's all."

"You weren't prepared, were you?" He shifted, and her cheek slipped against one of his shirt buttons. "For Milo and Nettie?"

"No." She wanted to sink into the strength of Joe's chest, stay there, not think about her dad and the kind woman he'd curled his arm around. "I think Pa started to warn me right before the party started, but we were sidetracked. The situation is probably as awkward for him as it is for me. Maybe more."

She lifted her head. "I'm being silly. I was surprised, that's all. I wasn't expecting Pa to have a—significant other." Her laugh felt rusty in her throat. "Gosh, that sounds so funny. My pa *dating.*"

"How long ago did your mom pass away, Gabby?"

At the back of her head, his fingers massaged her neck and she rested against their power, shutting her eyes.

"Over a year ago."

"I'm sorry. That must have been difficult."

"It was." She tightened her grip on his shirt. "Oh, Joe, I miss her every day. So much. I thought it would get easier. It doesn't. It only gets—different. A phrase I overhear while I'm shopping will remind me of her. I think I see her out of the corner of my eyes. I'll see a shadow in the corner, and I'll think she's there." She hesitated, continued. "I turn, ready to share the joke with her, a glitch in my brain making me forget that she's dead, and I *believe* she's right behind me." Memory stung her, a sharp pain that never seemed to vanish. "But she never is."

"Aw, sweet pea."

Gabrielle swallowed. "Mom would want Pa to be happy, to have someone to share his life with. I do, too." Her head tilted to each side as Joe worked out the stiffness in her neck. She hadn't realized she'd become so tense during the evening. "I must have realized something the minute Nettie arrived. Pa kept watching the door, but I thought he was excited about having the party again. Getting back to normal. Whatever normal is."

"This must be very tough for you. Missing your mom. And, in a way, losing your dad."

She went still. Seeing her dad with Nettie *had* felt like loss. That was the source of her pain. Another loss. Opening her eyes, she met Joe's, their golden brown depths wryly compassionate. "You're right. I don't know how you understand this, but you've nailed it. You must think I'm a selfish brat."

"I think you love your dad." Again his nimble fingers kneaded the muscles in her neck. "Hold still." He placed both thumbs along her jawbone and tipped her head back and forth, touching her chin to her chest and back, working out the last of the kinks. "And I think you're wired tighter than a Slinky toy."

"What?" With her head down, she focused on the tips of his glossy shoes. Nice shoes. Expensive shoes. "Slinky?"

He rolled her head back, resting it on his open palms and pressing against her temples with his busy fingers. "Didn't you have a Slinky when you were a bitty girl?"

"I don't remember. Maybe."

Once more he tipped her head forward. His shoes came into view as he moved his fingers to her shoulders, digging and smoothing until she thought she'd whimper with pleasure, her body relaxing and melting under his touch, her eyelids drifting closed. "You must have had a Slinky. Milo would have given you anything, I'll bet."

"Does Oliver have a Slinky?"

Joe checked the movement of his hands against her shoulders. "Beats me."

"You haven't been busy packing toys and finding Lego

pieces under your bare feet?" Raising her head, she stepped back, curious.

"No." Joe walked to the sink, looked out at the yard.

Under his shirt, the long muscles of his back defined his spine. "No, I haven't found Lego pieces underfoot. I wish to God I had." Turning abruptly toward her, he braced himself on the counter. "Gabby, I don't know much about my son."

"Why not?" She wondered at the intensity in Joe's expression. This was more serious than a man experiencing pangs of incompetency as a father. "Were you traveling a lot while he was growing up?"

"Oliver comes with a lot of baggage, but not a lot of possessions. No Lego. No stacks of books. No robot monsters. He has a blanket and a banged-up scrapbook with three pictures."

"I'm sorry, Joe. I don't understand." Gabrielle thought about the child who'd been so territorial about his tree, so possessive of his dad. "How could he not have *stuff*? Kids are pack rats. They all have stuff. They collect junk from the road. All kinds of gross things."

"Oliver doesn't. And, until three weeks ago, I was a man who had no idea he had a son." His knuckles were white as he clenched the sink rim. "An early Christmas present, you might say."

Delicately, picking her way through what she sensed was a difficult situation, and her heart going out to the pain she saw in Joe's face, Gabrielle asked, "You didn't know what? That Oliver existed? That he'd been born? What?"

"All of the above. He was living in an apartment in Chicago with a distant relative of his mother's."

"Your ex-wife?" She recalled that Joe had told her he wasn't married, but he hadn't said anything else.

"A woman I lived with seven years ago. She never told me about Oliver. I was careful, so I wouldn't have expected her to become pregnant."

"Oh." Gabrielle wondered about the woman who'd been with Joe, borne his child. Had Joe loved her? She must have loved him. Surely she had. "What happened?"

"His mother had left Oliver with the relative-by-marriage four years earlier. Walked out. Never came back. Oh, Jana called from time to time, enough to keep her relatives from calling the authorities. She sent the occasional check, too, and Suzie, the sort-of relative, liked kids, liked Oliver, and time passed. But Jana walked out on Oliver the same way she walked out of my life. The difference was that I wasn't a two-year-old baby. And I didn't care."

"You must have cared. A little."

"Lust. Propinquity. Opportunity. A seven-month version of a one-night stand, I reckon. Nothing more."

Gabrielle wasn't sure she believed him. Either way, his version of the story was bleak. No matter what anyone said about sex for sex's sake being fun, it was an emotional desert. She couldn't comprehend removing all emotion from an act that personal, that intense. "That's sad, Joe. Empty. For you. And I'd guess for Jana. But she must have loved Oliver in her own way. She sent checks to…Suzie? That means *something.*"

"Really?" His drawl was bitter. "Not much in Jana's case, that's for sure."

"Joe—" she shook his arm "—she was his *mother.* I'm sure she loved him. In her own way. How could she not?"

"Well, Gabby, it's your nature to look on the bright side, to expect the best out of people. But you didn't know Jana."

"True. Look, I'm no Pollyanna. I know that there's evil in the world. Don't sell me short. You may think I'm a naive, small-town girl still, but I'm not. I read the newspapers. I understand what can happen. It seems more credible to me that Jana had a compelling reason to walk away from Oliver."

Breaking loose in a sudden bark, his laugh was harsh. "Pleasure? Lack of interest?"

"Ah, Joe, that's so cynical. You knew her. If you didn't love her, you must have liked her, at least."

"Fair enough." Joe scrubbed his face hard, as if he were punishing himself. "The situation wasn't all her fault. I'll cop to that. I wasn't a man who was living up to anyone's expectations at that point in my life. Jana was—available. I was, too." He sighed heavily, the sound loud in the quiet kitchen. "And she made me laugh. Yes, I liked her. Until I found out about Oliver."

Gabrielle waited, thinking hard before she asked her next question. She didn't know Jana, but she knew Joe, knew him at some elemental level. He'd hinted he wasn't a candidate for Good Citizen of the Year, but every instinct in her body told her he wouldn't have abandoned a woman he was involved with. Not Joe. There were some facts missing. As carefully as she could phrase her question, she asked, "Why do you think she didn't tell you about Oliver?"

There was a long pause before Joe answered, his words coming slowly as if he were sifting through possibilities. "I can't answer that. Her behavior is a mystery to me. But I'm looking for answers. I would have married her, given her support money. Anything she needed. For the boy."

Gabrielle would bet a thousand dollars Joe had left something out, some fact he wasn't prepared to share. "So you'd never heard of him or seen him?"

"The day I strolled into that apartment was the first time I saw him." Joe's gaze was blazingly fierce as it fixed on her. "My son."

"How did you find him?" Gabrielle yearned to say something that would ease the tightness in his face. She couldn't imagine what that moment had been like. For both of them.

"Suzie had kept Oliver for four years, waiting for Jana to come back for him. She didn't. Once in a while a check arrived, but after Suzie hadn't had any money from Jana for almost a year, she couldn't afford to keep Oliver any longer.

It boggles my mind that she played mother for as long as she did. She has four kids of her own and no husband. Suzie has a kind heart, and she's a sucker for a sad tale. Jana must have played her along. At any rate, not hearing from Jana, Suzie was desperate. Going through some boxes of papers Jana had left in storage, she found my name and tracked me down. Jana had put my name on Oliver's birth certificate." His mouth thinned. "At least Jana had enough sense of responsibility to do that. But I'm amazed Suzie found me. That address was seven years old. The apartment where Jana and I had lived for a while."

"What if Suzie hadn't found you?"

"She'd planned to call the Department of Child Welfare after Christmas. Oliver would have gone into the system." Joe slowly lifted his shoulders, as if moving them took all his strength. "I would never have found him. That's what almost happened."

"How horrible." In one quick step, Gabrielle was at his side, her hand curling over his hand that still gripped the sink rim with such force she wondered the porcelain didn't shatter. "He's with you permanently? His mother surrendered custody?"

"I hired a private investigator. He found Jana. She'd been killed in a drive-by shooting down in Gary, Indiana. She was living with some man under a different name. Nobody connected Jane Stakowski from Gary with Jana Stanley, who'd abandoned a small boy in Chicago."

"Oh, Joe. Poor Oliver. No wonder he clings to you the way he does. I'm amazed he hasn't been at your side this whole evening, in fact."

"He's attached himself to Cletis and your dad, but he keeps his eye on the kitchen door. He checks to see that I'm in here. That I haven't gone strolling out the back door. He and Cletis poke a finger and a paw through the door on a regular basis. Haven't you seen it crack open?"

"I missed that. After all that's happened, he must be terrified you'll disappear, too." Gabrielle rubbed her cheek against the sleeve of his shirt.

"He trusts me. For some crazy, illogical reason, the little guy trusts *me*. Never saw me before, and he strolled out of that apartment as if he'd been with me all his life. Didn't even blink. Nuts, huh?"

"Sure. Silly kid. Trusting you like that. What's the matter with him, anyway?" A tear slipped from her eye and dampened his sleeve. She rubbed her eyes dry on the smooth cotton. She didn't have the right to inflict her distress on Joe. Not after what Oliver had endured. Surreptitiously, she wiped her eyes again. She wasn't involved. She was a bystander in Joe and Oliver's lives, on the fringes. As she now was in her dad's life. Her dad had moved on. She hadn't.

Through the lustrous fabric of his shirt, she felt the hard muscles of Joe's arm bunching and tensing. Like a string drawn tight on a bow, his whole body leaned forward, only the most enormous discipline keeping him from lashing out with his fist and smashing something.

Someone.

But there was no one to smash, no way to change the past, to *fix* the terrible wrong. No villains, at least none that she saw.

Still, thinking of Oliver cast adrift on the seas of chance, Gabrielle wanted to smash something herself. No child should be tossed out like tissue. Oliver deserved more from life. His stubborn independence and sturdiness demanded recognition. Against all odds, he'd survived. Oh, not merely physically, but emotionally. The scars were there, sure, but he'd survived. And so had Joe.

Like father, like son. Two peas in a pod, as her mama used to say.

For a long moment she and Joe stayed silent, side by side,

the rhythm of his breathing matching hers, breath for slow, even breath.

The oddly tranquil moment had a rightness to it that confused her, comforted her, made her yearn for something she couldn't quite identify.

The door slammed against the wall. "Are we going to starve out here, or what?" Moon's big face preceded the bulk of his body as he leaned through the door and stopped as he saw them side by side, her arm resting on Joe's. "What's going on, folks? Spreading a little Christmas cheer of your own?"

"Mind your business, Moon." Joe straightened slowly, an alertness in the muscles under her hand, his stance that of an animal ready to attack. Or defend.

He was worried about *her,* about her reputation.

"Actually, Moon, for your information, I was flirting with Joe. You've interrupted us in the throes of passion. I confess. You caught us." She batted her eyelashes theatrically at Joe and felt the tension in him ease.

"Oh, right, Gabrielle. You and Joe. Sure. And you have that swell piece of property along the gulf that you're willing to sell me for next to nothing. Like I'd believe that story." Moon's laugh was full-bellied. "Good one. Anyway, when are we going to eat, girl?" His face turned pitiful. "I'm starving. I need food. I'm a growing boy."

"Lord, I hope not." Joe strolled over to him, punched him on the shoulder. "If you grew any more, you'd shake the house to pieces with every step, old son."

"Don't 'old son' me, you cycle-riding hooligan." Laughing, Moon punched him back, a playful swipe at Joe's arm and shoulder, but a bearlike thwack all the same.

Joe didn't flinch.

Gabrielle was impressed. The punch had been hard enough, even in fun, to rock most men back on their heels. She'd been aware of Joe's muscled body under his civilized suit and shirt, but she was amazed by his toughness in the face of Moon's enthusiastic whomp on the shoulder.

Seeing her astonishment, Joe said, "Relax. Moon and I like each other."

"Yeah." Moon nodded vigorously. "Joe's not half bad. For a short, underfed specimen."

Gabrielle's gaze drifted to Joe's sinewy six feet, then returned to Moon. "Gosh, I really enjoy the way guys express affection. All that pounding and whacking at each other. So what do you do when you're ticked off with each other?"

Moon and Joe exchanged glances.

"Women. They don't get it, do they, Moon?"

"Nope," Moon added agreeably. "But I *really* need to get some food, Gabrielle. I'm not fooling."

"All right, Moon. I suppose I ought to have pity on you. Carry the news back to the troops. The next round of food is on the way."

"Damn, it sure smells good." Moon lifted the lid on the pot, reaching in with one thick finger. "Did Milo make enough?"

"For you, or for everyone else?" She smacked his hand with the wooden spoon. "There's this pot, and the one staying warm in the oven. Think that will be enough? One pot for you, one for the rest of the guests?" Behind her, Joe cleared his throat with amusement.

"Aw, Gabrielle, don't be mean. I can't help myself. I love Milo's cooking." Moon threw a heavy arm around her shoulder, and she staggered momentarily under the weight.

"Come on, Moon. You and I can haul out the jambalaya. Okay, Gabby?" Joe lifted Moon's arm off her shoulders and handed him a pair of Santa Claus pot holders. "Grab the handles, Moon. I'll get the door and the other batch. Heads up, sweet pea." Joe's grin whipped across his face, a blaze of white teeth and satisfaction.

In an exaggerated bend and stoop, she dodged as Moon

swung the massive pot off the stove and headed for the door. "I'll bring the salad bowl." She poked Joe in the ribs as he opened the oven door and lifted out the second pot. "And behave yourself."

"More fun not to."

"You're a bad boy, Joe Carpenter."

"Of course," he said smugly.

"But only some of the time," she added softly.

As Moon backed through the door and out of hearing range, Joe murmured, "Thanks. For listening." His eyes didn't meet hers, and a narrow flush touched his cheekbones.

"Anytime." She hit him on the shoulder. "There. Guy-style communication." She regarded her fist thoughtfully. "Hey, there might be something to this. Efficient, at least. Once you get the hang of it. A kind of one-style-fits-all communication."

"Better ways of communicating. Between a man and a woman, that is." His grin was all masculine provocation. "And, Gabby?"

"Yes?" She gave him the prissiest look she could muster.

"In case you're wondering, I'm flirting with you."

"I know. And, Joe?"

"Yes, sweet pea?"

"I'm flirting back." She swished her skirt at him.

"Okay." The door shut quietly as he, too, backed out, following Moon.

Everything inside her loosened and relaxed. All the questions about Milo and Nettie, the distress over Oliver's situation, her confusion about the way she felt around Joe—everything smoothed out as she thought about the look on Joe's face as he'd teased her. An inexplicable affection there, underneath the gleam, an affection that reached right down inside her, fluttering her tummy.

In the dining room, the sideboard and dining table were loaded with bowls and platters of food. Under the dangling edge of the tablecloth, she saw a furry gray paw reach out to slap at Taylor Padgett's ankle as he leaned over the table to spear a smoked oyster.

"Watch it, Taylor. You're being stalked." The salad bowl in her hands, Gabrielle pointed with her elbow.

"You scared the heck out of me for a moment. Surgeons don't like to hear that word." He shuddered. "These days that could mean a dissatisfied patient."

"I hear you do good work, Taylor." Gabrielle set the bowl on the buffet across from the sideboard. Moon and Joe had already placed the white pots of jambalaya at each end. Earlier in the day, she'd arranged the red-and-white Christmas dishes on the buffet, their faded trees and tinted gold stars giving her pleasure.

"I like to believe that. But you've heard the rap on us surgeons. We think we're one miracle away from God." He raised his eyebrows, offering her the chance to make fun at his expense. "And sometimes it's true."

"But remember, Taylor, I knew you back when." She stuck her tongue out at him. "Hard to create God-like awe in someone who's seen you skinny-dipping with your college girlfriend."

He grimaced. "Oh, yes. I remember. Bad day at Black Rock, so to speak. And not nice of you to remind me. Alas, a prophet without honor in his own country. Maybe I should think about that offer from Atlanta Medical. *They* think I'm hot stuff."

"Having seen you 'buck-nekkid,' as Pa would say, I have trouble agreeing with them." She laughed as he sputtered cracker crumbs tableward. "But don't expect me to apologize. Heck, you paid off in soda pop for the rest of the summer. Anyway, Taylor, reminiscences aside, I haven't had a chance to talk with you since I came home. I haven't heard any complaints from Pa, but he's not saying much about his surgery."

Crunching an oyster-laden cracker, Taylor ambled over to

her. He brushed cracker crumbs off the lapels of his brown jacket. "Milo did quite well."

"You don't think he looks tired?" She brushed away a crumb that had caught on his sleeve. "Because I do."

Taylor swiveled his head until he located Milo in the midst of a group in the living room, Nettie Drew beside him. Taylor watched for a minute. "He looks one hundred per cent to me, Gabrielle. That infection he developed after he left the hospital—"

"Pa didn't mention an infection."

"No?" Cracker crumbs dribbled into his mustache.

She shook her head. She'd been right to come home. Milo *was* ill. "This is the first I've heard of an infection."

"It wasn't serious. I stay on top of complicating factors like postoperative infection. Milo called as soon as he popped a fever, and we caught it early. Milo's fine."

"I worry about him, Taylor." Gabrielle took his hand and held it. "He's not telling me everything. I'm scared that something else is wrong with him. That you didn't get all the tumor. I worry."

Taylor covered her hand reassuringly. "Hey, kiddo, don't insult my work. I've got ten years on you, and remember, I kid-sat you for a spell while you were in diapers, so you have to show me proper respect. I'm good. Best in the area, in fact. Milo is fine, Gabrielle. Trust me." He patted her hand. "You don't have to worry about him. Enjoy Christmas. Have a cup of glogg. You won't worry about anything after half a cup of that brew."

"Doctor's orders?"

"You bet. Drink up, kiddo. The night's still young." Giving her a hug, he wandered toward the crowd in the living room.

She would have a cup, too. Maybe even two.

This was what she'd wanted when she left Arizona. Everybody around her, the house loud with merriment.

Tradition.

This was the way Christmas was supposed to be. She could let the richness of being home envelop her. She wouldn't give in to this nagging worry about her dad.

Taylor would have given her a hint, a clue, if anything were wrong with Milo.

She frowned. Wouldn't he?

In the living room, the tree, no longer ugly, shone with tiny Italian lights and ornaments, some of which had come down from her great-grandparents. The salt-dough angel she'd made with her mother years ago and sprinkled extravagantly with blue glitter hung heavily from one skinny branch.

After supper, her dad would hang the crystal star. It symbolized the magic of Christmas for her, its crystal glinting softly in the dark. Old and fragile, the star had come from Ireland, a souvenir of her grandmother, her mother's mother, whose powdery scent clung to Gabrielle whenever she cuddled on her grandmother's lap.

A link from the past to the present, rich with memories.

Gabrielle remembered taking the star down from the tree that last time with her mother and wrapping it carefully in tissue. Sipping orange tea, they'd laughed about the holidays and toasted each other, "To next Christmas!" Christmas over for another year, her mother had laid the star gently in its own special box and rubbed her head.

It was their last Christmas together.

The lights on the tree blurred into a shimmer of white.

Suddenly, a claw snagged her ankle, catching her nylons. "Hey, Cletis." She stooped and scratched the cat's ears. "Where's your buddy?"

The tablecloth pooched, billowed out.

"Here." The edge of the tablecloth framed Oliver's face. His cheeks were bright red and he was slightly sweaty. His hair had thrown off the constraints of whatever Joe had put on it.

"Hungry?" Picking up Cletis and tucking his chunky head

under her chin, Gabrielle wandered slowly in Oliver's direction, stopping to collect a rolled-up sliver of smoked mullet Moon had brought. Cletis poked his head into her face and kept pushing at her chin until she shared a nibble with him.

"Me and Cletis have been eating."

"I can tell," she said seriously.

Inch by inch, Oliver crept out from the protection of the tablecloth. "And drinking."

"Oh? What did you have?" She put Cletis down as he head-butted her again. "Sorry, mister, the mullet's gone."

"Milo gave me punch. It's red. With frozen strawberries. He said that other stuff is bitter. He let me lick the spoon. I didn't like it. But the red stuff's okay."

"Good." She breathed a sigh of relief. For an instant she'd been afraid Oliver had been nipping glogg. "Want to come with me to the living room? We'll tell everybody soup's on."

"I don't like soup."

"It's not really soup. That's an expression that means it's time to eat."

He stood, rear end angling skyward as he wiped his hands down his pants. On the bottom of his dangling shirttails, red stains sent a festive message. "I can tell everyone?"

"Sure. Can you speak loudly enough so everyone can hear you?"

He rolled his eyes. "Of course." He reached for Cletis, who had waddled under his own steam beneath the table toward safety.

Gabrielle suspected Cletis—and Oliver—had their own stash of munchies hidden under the table.

The cat's belly hung in folds as Oliver hoisted him up, grunting. "Me and Cletis will tell everybody soup's on. Even if it's not soup." He marched toward the living room and stood in the archway between the two rooms. "Soup's on!" he bellowed, and then led the parade to the dining room.

Joe stood aside, letting people tromp past him. Everyone

was pairing up, couples, friends, lining up for food and making their way to corners and end tables where they could eat and visit.

He didn't know anyone except Moon and Gabby. And Milo, of course.

Maybe this would be a good time to leave. He and Oliver, who'd clearly been stuffing himself all evening, could slip out the door.

No one would even know they'd gone.

No one would miss them.

Milo waved his hands, directing people to both sides of the table. "Y'all come on. Moon, help me shag this crew toward the food. All this sudden bashfulness sure seems suspicious to me. Y'all sure you're the same group I see around town every day?" Laughter greeted Milo's words as he placed a hand at Nettie Drew's waist and led her in, while Moon was at the back of the line of guests.

"What do you expect, Milo? We're all squashed into our party duds. Have to behave when you have a tie choking you."

"Hell's bells, Dial. We've seen your damned tie. Stick it in your pocket and eat," Moon groused. "Don't hold up the line, man. Some of us are desperate back here."

"Right, folks. And you sure don't want to be in Moon's way when the notion takes him to eat." Milo motioned for them to make a path for Moon.

Joe watched Gabrielle walk over to Taylor Padgett and tuck his arm into hers, leading him toward the dining room. He was the surgeon, a man she'd grown up with. A family friend. Why wouldn't she make a point of ushering him in first? Well, not first. Oliver and Cletis had taken care of that. Joe could understand Gabby's interest in the doctor.

After all, he had standing in the community, respect. He was the perfect man for Gabby. Unencumbered with burdens from the past, Taylor Padgett could give her the kind of life she was used to.

The kind of life Gabrielle O'Shea deserved.

Joe wished the idea gave him more satisfaction. Surprised, he looked down to see his clenched fist. Slowly unclenching his fingers, he stuck his hand in his pocket and reminded himself once more of Padgett's sterling qualities.

Much better to think of those sterling qualities than to imagine smashing in the doctor's carefully groomed, mustached face.

Unfortunately, Padgett's sterling qualities were all too easy to find. The man was the next best thing to a saint. Everyone in town had made a point of mentioning how wonderful Doc Padgett was.

Sourly, he had to admit Taylor Padgett did seem like an all-around, hell of a fine fellow. Shoot, he even liked Padgett himself. What wasn't to like?

The only problem with Padgett was that he was next to Gabby and Joe wasn't.

She sure seemed enthralled by the man.

If Padgett stepped any closer, the man would be wearing her for his very own lapel pin.

At some intellectual level, Joe found his very primal reaction to the doctor amusing. This visceral urge to pin the man's ears back was unexpected. He couldn't ever recall feeling so— protective about a woman. So possessive.

And that thought shocked him most of all.

Because he wanted to be Gabby's friend, not her lover.

He hadn't realized how much he'd needed a friend until she stood at his side and listened as he sorted out the crazy mess of his feelings. There had been no one before her he'd wanted to tell about Oliver, and how Joe had found the boy.

Sometimes a man needed a woman friend, someone he could talk with about confusing thoughts and feelings. Sex complicated things between a man and a woman.

Every damned time.

He didn't want the complication of sex in his life, not sex with Gabby, anyway.

She was different.

Sex would destroy the fragile bonds of friendship they were developing. That awareness was what they'd both danced around with their discussion about flirting. They could flirt and be friends. They couldn't have sex and remain friends.

He knew Gabby wasn't the type of woman who could separate sex from her emotions.

Flirting was one thing. Sex another.

Being ticked off with Padgett went beyond the boundaries of friendship. Coiling inside Joe, that emotion had to do with sex, not friendship.

He wanted friendship.

But, hell, he still wished he was the man standing that close to Gabby, not Padgett.

That was the way of the world. Water sought its own level.

He knew that, had accepted it long before he moved to Bayou Bend, but he'd never before been so ticked off at a really nice guy, a swell fellow who didn't have a clue that Joe was happily fantasizing ways to get rid of him.

As the very wonderful doc leaned and spoke into Gabby's ear, she laughed, a light, lovely sound that came to him and left him feeling as alone as he'd ever been in his life.

Outside, looking in.

Where he'd always been.

Then, at the exact second Joe felt like a kid with his nose pressed up against the toy shop window, Gabby turned and smiled at him, strolling back through the crowd to stand next to him.

"Hey, Joe, come join the party. Oliver has a head start on you. I think he's staked out his spot under the table with the cat. We'll find you a place." Slipping her arm through Joe's, her palm sliding over his forearm, she led him into the dining room.

Funny, the word she'd used, he thought as she tugged him forward, making room in the crowd for him.

His *place.*

He wished he knew what his place was in Bayou Bend. Once upon a time he'd understood exactly what his place here was and had run away like a wild child. But now, could he find a *place* for himself and Oliver?

Gabby seemed determined to find one for him.

He wasn't used to having someone look after him.

Her concern tickled him, warmed him faster than the glogg Moon pressed into his hand.

Maybe Doc Padgett didn't hold all the cards.

Question was, though, could a man be friends with Gabby O'Shea and keep sex out of his thoughts?

Maybe.

Maybe not.

Joe let his fingers slip down to close around hers.

Together, they entered the dining room.

Chapter Six

Joe knew exactly how he came to be seated with Milo, Nettie and Gabby.

With her skill at maneuvering people, she could have been a general. Padgett wound up with Moon and three nurses Milo had invited from the hospital, Oliver and Cletis lay stretched out on their overstuffed bellies under the table, and Joe, miracle of miracles, found himself with Gabby curled up on the floor next to him, her hair clinging to the fabric of his slacks.

"You like Pa's cooking, Joe?" she asked drowsily, placing the mug of glogg on the floor beside her. Lifting out the cinnamon stick, she licked off the last drops and let the curled twig fall back into the mug. Her cheeks were pink-tinged, and her eyes all soft and dreamy. "He does a pretty good job, doesn't he, this old man of mine?"

Hearing her, Milo turned to them. "Only one correct answer, Carpenter. This is a test, you know. Wrong answer, you don't get dessert."

"I usually get my just deserts, Milo. You know that." It was the closest Joe would allow himself to touch the subject of that night years ago. He wanted Milo to know he remembered, that he hadn't forgotten what Milo had done.

Placing her hand on Joe's knee to steady her, Gabby shifted. Her touch burned right through the fabric. "Joe," she repeated sleepily, "you didn't answer."

"Milo's jambalaya is fit for a king."

"Joe, why don't you and I have coffee one morning soon?" Not looking in Joe's direction, Milo handed Nettie a shrimp from his own plate. Offhand, casual, the question attracted no attention.

But Joe heard the message in the invitation and was relieved. He and Milo needed to air out the past. "Good idea. I'll have to work out sitter arrangements for Oliver and get back to you."

Gabby yawned, the pink tip of her tongue catching his attention. "Oliver can stay with me. I'm planning on making cookies tomorrow. Maybe he'd like that. He can help me. If not, we'll go shopping." She stretched her arms and yawned again. "We'll figure out something. An adventure. After I clean up whatever mess is left from tonight." She shook her head, and a feathery strand of hair floated against his hand.

Such power in that light touch, power to make him want. To hope for impossible things.

But reality was built, brick by brick, from what was possible.

He stirred, and her hair settled against her cheek, a shiny brown line against pink.

"Sounds like a plan," Milo said. "We can meet tomorrow. Nine o'clock too early, honey?"

"Pa, usually I've done half a day's work by nine. I believe I can drag myself to the flour canister by that time of day." Resting her hand again on Joe's knee, her breath puffing warm and damp against his leg, she added, "Check with Oliver first, though, all right?"

A less-controlled man would have hauled her straight into

his lap. Joe didn't. Without making an issue of Oliver's situation, she'd solved it. Gabby knew how Oliver might react to Joe's heading off somewhere. That was why he'd waited to return to work until after Christmas. His business could be put on hold for a little while.

Longer if Oliver had trouble settling in to this new school.

"You not working tomorrow, Joe?" Milo's casual question shouldn't have pushed a button, but it did.

Joe knew what Milo was after. Details. Milo's lawyerly instincts, picking and nailing everything down. "Nope."

"No time clock to punch?"

"Nope." Joe didn't think it would hurt Milo to wait for information until they had their meeting. He didn't want to explain everything in front of Gabby, not unless he had to. Eventually he would tell her everything.

But not yet.

Not until he'd settled Oliver in.

"Speaking of Oliver, honey, what would you think if we let Oliver stick the star on top of the tree?" Milo's voice was low, almost as if he didn't see Oliver and Cletis crawling on their bellies toward them. "Okay with you, Joe?"

The question had a weight to it he didn't quite catch, but he understood that for the O'Sheas, topping the tree with this star was an important moment. If the star was that important, maybe Oliver shouldn't be involved. Uncomfortable, feeling like an outsider suddenly thrust into the spotlight, Joe started to stop the snowball before it rolled downhill. "I don't—"

"Sure, Pa. I think that would be a wonderful idea." Gabby's voice trembled as she interrupted Joe.

Looking sharply at her, he felt his uneasiness increase. This star thing was significant. A low profile seemed much more appealing to him as father and daughter waited for his answer.

"I think Oliver would like that, Joe," Gabby murmured huskily. "Ask him." Tucking her legs under her, yoga-style, she bent forward, her back stretching out all gold and slippery as she rested her elbows on the floor. Her hair fanned around her shoulders, light brown against gold shimmer as she spoke to Oliver. "Wouldn't you?"

Facing her, nose to nose, his son gazed steadily at Gabrielle. "I don't know."

"Putting up the star is a tradition for us. It means—oh, Oliver, it means Christmas is around the corner. It means we're all together. Family. Friends. Together."

"Does it mean Santa Claus will know how to find you?"

"Yes," she answered, solemnly, drowsily, "it means that, too. It shines so everyone can find their way home, Oliver."

"I want to hang the star." Oliver tugged on Joe's hand. "Okay?"

Glancing at Milo and Gabby, Joe tried to read their expressions, to see if there were any reason his son shouldn't participate in this small ceremony.

Finding no clues to help him, he yielded to the second, imperceptible tug. "Please, Daddy?"

Gabby caught Oliver's attention. "I'll get the star, and tomorrow, Oliver, if you help me make cookies, I'll tell you the story about the woman who brought this crystal star all the way from Ireland."

"Crystal? Magic? Like with the robots on TV?"

"Crystal, yes. Magic, definitely. But I don't know about the TV robots."

"'Cause you're too old, probably," he said matter-of-factly, and trotted to the living room, Cletis lumbering behind him.

"I think your cat has adopted my son."

"Or vice versa."

"You don't know about TV robots, huh? Even I know that much." He tsk-tsked. "I feel awful bad for you, age creeping up on you like this."

"I know. I'm a pitiful case. I can hear the creaking joints right now." Gabby stood up, swayed, and Joe caught her el-

WELCOME TO THE
CASINO!

Try your luck at the Roulette Wheel ...
Play a hand of Twenty-One!

How to play:

1. Play the Roulette and Twenty-One scratch-off games, as instructed on the opposite page, to see that you are eligible for FREE BOOKS and a FREE GIFT!

2. Send back the card and you'll receive TWO brand-new Silhouette Romance® novels. These books have a cover price of $3.50 each, but they are yours to keep absolutely free.

3. There's no catch. You're under no obligation to buy anything. We charge nothing — ZERO — for your first shipment. And you don't have to make any minimum number of purchases — not even one!

4. The fact is, thousands of readers enjoy receiving books by mail from the Silhouette Reader Service™ before they're available in stores. They like the convenience of home delivery, and they love our discount prices!

5. We hope that after receiving your free books you'll want to remain a subscriber. But the choice is yours — to continue or cancel, any time at all!

So why not take us up on our invitation, with no risk of any kind. You'll be glad you did!

Play Twenty-One For This Exquisite Free Gift!

THIS SURPRISE MYSTERY GIFT COULD BE YOURS FREE WHEN YOU PLAY
TWENTY-ONE

It's fun, and we're giving away **FREE GIFTS** to all players!

PLAY ROULETTE!

Scratch the silver to see where the ball has landed—7 RED or 11 BLACK makes you eligible for TWO FREE romance novels!

PLAY TWENTY-ONE!

Scratch the silver to reveal a winning hand! Congratulations, you have Twenty-One. Return this card promptly and you'll receive a fabulous free mystery gift, along with your free books!

YES!

Please send me all the free Silhouette Romance® books and the gift for which I qualify! I understand that I am under no obligation to purchase any books, as explained on the back of this card.

Name (please print clearly)
_____

Address _____ Apt.# _____

City _____ State _____ Zip _____

Offer limited to one per household and not valid to current Silhouette Romance® subscribers. All orders subject to approval. PRINTED IN U.S.A.

(U-SIL-R-12/98)   **215 SDL CKFJ**

The Silhouette Reader Service™ — Here's how it works:

Accepting free books places you under no obligation to buy anything. You may keep the books and gift and return the shipping statement marked "cancel." If you do not cancel, about a month later we'll send you 6 additional novels and bill you just $2.90 each, plus 25¢ delivery per book and applicable sales tax, if any.* That's the complete price — and compared to cover prices of $3.50 each — quite a bargain! You may cancel at any time, but if you choose to continue, every month we'll send you 6 more books, which you may either purchase at the discount price...or return to us and cancel your subscription.

*Terms and prices subject to change without notice. Sales tax applicable in N.Y.

If offer card is missing write to: Silhouette Reader Service, 3010 Walden Ave., P.O. Box 1867, Buffalo, NY 14240-9952

BUSINESS REPLY MAIL

FIRST-CLASS MAIL   PERMIT NO 717   BUFFALO NY

POSTAGE WILL BE PAID BY ADDRESSEE

SILHOUETTE READER SERVICE
3010 WALDEN AVE
PO BOX 1867
BUFFALO NY 14240-9952

NO POSTAGE
NECESSARY
IF MAILED
IN THE
UNITED STATES

bow, steadying her. Looking down at his hand cradling her arm, she said, "This is turning into a habit."

"Not one that has to be broken," he said as she leaned into him.

"What habit's that?" Milo stood up and held out a helping hand to Nettie. "Who needs to break bad habits?"

"We all do, Milo." Nettie's gentle comment had Gabby turning to her.

"Not a bad habit. I ran into Oliver and Joe at Moon's tree lot yesterday. Joe kept me from falling flat on my face in the mud."

"A good man to have around," Nettie said, following them. "When there's heavy-going."

Joe hesitated. Where had Nettie's kindness come from? Did she have any idea what that casual comment meant to him? She couldn't, of course, but her easy words smoothed some rough, raw spot inside him.

"Where's the star?" Oliver stood by the tree, ragtag and the worse for wear.

Joe groaned as Gabby retrieved a camera from a shelf and squinted through it.

Pictures.

Would this be a memory Oliver would want to keep in that scrapbook with his three pictures? Would it, too, curl and dim under the pressure of his son's fingers tracing the faces?

"Here's the O'Shea star." Milo sat on the sun-faded couch and motioned for Oliver to come over. "Listen," Milo whispered, and flicked his finger against the crystal.

The clear, pure *ping* made Oliver inhale. "Oh," he murmured, and leaned against Milo, enthralled.

"See, Oliver, how this hollow center will go over the point of the tree top?" The crystal shone, catching the reflection of the lights in the room, shooting rays of light back.

Oliver nodded, his eyes huge and dark. "And it will shine and anybody can find you."

"Right. Joe, you want to lift your boy up so he can stick the star up there? Right on the tippy-top."

Joe lifted his little son. Body shaking, Oliver clipped an arm around Joe's neck. "I'm going to put the *star* on the tree, Daddy," he whispered in awe. "I *never* done that before. The *Christmas* star."

Milo handed Joe the ornament, Gabby squinted through the camera, and Joe handed the crystal star to Oliver, who leaned forward and reached with both hands for the lovely piece of Irish workmanship.

A flash popped, Nettie laughed, and then, so fast Joe could only stretch out his hand, the crystal slipped through Oliver's hands and tumbled, end over end, sparkles of light flashing and shining as it fell.

Shards of crystal twinkled at Joe's feet.

The stunned silence in the room was the loudest sound he'd ever heard.

His son's cry was the most wrenching.

"Daddy!" Oliver screamed, and buried his head in the crook of Joe's neck. "I killed it, I killed the star!" His sobs were wrenching, deep and horrible.

Sorrow filling him, Joe clutched his son and whispered, "It's okay, Oliver. It's all right. You didn't kill it." As Oliver's sobs subsided to a steady, quiet racking of his small body, Joe lifted his head and glared at the assembled adults, daring them to—what?

Say something?

React with outrage?

Call the cops?

He didn't know, but no one was going to hurt his son with careless words, not over some damned trinket, even if it was the O'Shea Irish star and cost the earth.

Her scent came to him first, and suddenly Gabrielle stood beside him. Wrapping her arms around Oliver, she pressed her face against his shaking shoulder. "Shh, sweetie. Your daddy's right. You didn't kill it. It's only glass." Her eyes were shining with tears as she clung to his son, but she kept murmuring to Oliver, telling him over and over that no one was angry with him, that everything would be okay. "It was an accident, sweetie. Accidents happen to everybody."

"But I killed the star!" Oliver hiccuped and sobbed uncontrollably, tears smearing his cheeks. "I ruined Christmas!"

"No, you didn't," Gabby whispered, her voice catching. "You couldn't. Christmas is people. People make the magic, Oliver. Not things. Listen, sweetie, we'll find something else to put on top of the tree. You and I can talk about that tomorrow when we're baking cookies. If you decide that's what you want to do."

"I want the star back," he wailed. "I want Christmas."

"Milo, Gabby, I think it's time for us to leave. It's late. Oliver's overtired." Sweat pouring down his back, Joe ached to get Oliver safely away, ached to make his son's world right again.

He wondered if he could.

He had no magic to heal a little boy's heart.

And there was Gabby, tears trembling in her eyes, her face pale and devastated.

Damage here, serious damage, to both Gabrielle and his son.

"Gabby, I'll call you about—well, you know." Joe gestured vaguely toward the glass glittering against the hardwood floor. "I'm—sorry."

"Joe, it's nothing. Please, don't worry about it." Still tear-filled, her eyes met his. "I don't want Oliver to lose any sleep over—over a bauble, hear me? And that's *all* it is. Was. A bauble."

As she spoke, everyone moved, scattered, leaving them alone. Over Oliver's shoulder, Joe saw the back of Milo's head.

Stopping under the arch between the two rooms, Milo

looked back, his face gray, his eyes as devastated as Gabby's. "Hey, squirt?"

Oliver burrowed his face into Joe. Joe braced himself, ready to do battle for his child, even with an old man, his host.

Cracking, Milo's voice carried into the stillness. "You listen to me, Oliver, because I'm a whole lot older. I'm supposed to be wiser, too. Sometimes. You listening, young man?"

The burrowing halted.

"You're a good boy. I was honored to have you put our star on the tree. If I had it to do over, I'd hand that star right back to you. *You,* no one else. Got it?"

Oliver's nod was imperceptible. Joe didn't know if Milo could see the tiny movement.

"Now, you go on back to the hotel with your dad. Get a good night's sleep. Tomorrow, you'll see. Christmas hasn't been ruined." Milo's shoulders were stooped, and the energy that had driven him throughout the evening seemed dimmed as Joe watched him try to console the small boy. "See you in the morning, Oliver."

"I'll walk you and Oliver to your car, Joe. Give me a minute, okay?" Gabby patted Oliver on the back once more and hurried after her father, her narrow shoulders slumped.

"Fine." In Joe's arms, Oliver went limp with a shudder, laying his head on Joe's tear-damp shoulder. Calling after her, Joe said, "My suit coat's in the kitchen. I threw it on one of the chairs. I'll get Oliver's jacket."

Striding to the closet near the front door, Joe shifted Oliver to a dry shoulder. "How you doing, my man? You okay?"

"'Kay."

Joe worked Oliver's arms into the sleeves of his new jacket and grabbed his own suit coat from Gabby, stuffing it under his arm as he headed for the door.

"Joe, slow down." She tagged the back of his shirt.

He didn't want to look at Gabby, didn't want to talk to her. Even though she and Milo had minimized the situation, it was clear that the star had been more to her family than a piece of crystal. Through him, harm had come to Oliver. To Milo. To Gabby.

He should have heeded that initial sense of discomfort.

Should have known better than to come here. Should have known better than to let his guard down and forget. He didn't belong here, and neither did his son. No matter how Gabrielle O'Shea pretended otherwise.

"Really, Joe, everything is fine." Forcing him to halt, she pushed at his side until he faced her. "You and Oliver are *not* to give this a second thought," she said fiercely, poking him in the side. "And if you don't get that gloom-and-doom expression off your face, I'll never speak to you again."

Another solid jab between his ribs.

Hand on the doorknob, Joe said, "I hear you, Gabrielle. And my ribs are going to be bruised for a week." Twisting the knob, he sought for words. "I understand what you're trying to do, believe me. I appreciate the effort and the intent. But—" He stopped as Oliver's foot twitched against his waist. "This was a mistake. Anyway, thanks. We'll head to my car now. Better if you stay with your guests." He opened the door and stepped out into the night, grateful for the darkness and the cool air. Behind him, the screen door clattered shut.

He had one foot on the porch step.

"Don't run away, Joe." Quiet as star music, her voice came to him. "You don't have to. I want you to stay." Blurred by the screen mesh, her face, drawn and serene, was backlit by the lights from inside the house. Lumped at her feet, Cletis watched lazily as she touched the mesh. "You were our guest, too."

"Yeah. Thanks."

Her smile wobbled. "And you don't have to keep saying 'thanks.' Repeating yourself, you are. Picking up my bad habits, Joe."

"I don't know what else to say, Gabrielle." Helpless to

explain the evening's impact, he shrugged. "Go back inside. Where you belong." Softening the bluntness, he added, "It's chilly. You'll catch your death."

Her laugh was nothing more than a sigh of sound, wistful and lonely, and her hair floated like the clouds around the moon, all gauzy and lit with light. "My mama used to say that to me all the time."

"Go inside, sweet pea." He took the two steps in one stride and placed his free hand flat against the screen over hers. Through the scratchy mesh her skin was warm under his.

Her fingernails scrabbled against his palm. "Good night, Joe."

"Good night, Gabrielle."

"See you in the morning, Oliver." Her palm slipped past Joe's.

"'Kay" came the muffled answer.

During the drive back to the hotel, Oliver fell asleep, his head slumping onto the car door, the car seat keeping him upright. Joe pressed the button to lower the window slightly on the driver's side. Like a tranquil touch from an unseen hand, the cool, damp air blew against his face.

He would find some way to salvage Gabby's heirloom star. Hell, he had an importer friend in New York who made regular trips to Ireland. They could find a duplicate. A replacement. She would feel better.

And Oliver would see that problems could be solved, that the world didn't end with a mistake, with an accident.

The scent of oranges, pungent and sharp, drifted in with the damp air.

The replacement wouldn't be the star that had broken.

That was gone. Even Tommy Boyle couldn't possibly find a substitute for that lovely thing before Christmas.

Gabrielle swept up the bits of glass onto the dustpan. Tilting it, she let the chips and shards flow in a rainbow of colors into the original cardboard box.

"Honey, I'm sorrier than I can tell you," Milo said as he watched her. "Because I came up with a damn fool idea, I made you and Oliver miserable. The kid got to me, though, the way he and Cletis hid out and watched all of us, the little guy noticing everything with those big brown eyes and not bothering a soul. Every now and then, he'd check on Joe, then scoot back under the table. I thought the boy would enjoy having a special moment. Something to remember. I made a terrible misjudgment. Can you forgive a damn fool old man?"

"Pa, I'll survive." She blew her nose in the tissue he handed her. "It's a wonder the star lasted as long as it did. Any kind of bump could have shattered it. I'm surprised no one's dropped it before. I mean, sixty-three years. It's—it *was* almost as old as you." She couldn't find a smile, no matter how she struggled. "But, oh, Pa, I sure wish it had been one of us who'd dropped it instead of that poor child. What a burden for him. His sobs broke my heart. No matter what we said, he kept blaming himself. He took it so hard." She blew her nose again.

"I know, honey, I know. My heart went out to him, too. And to Joe. He looked like someone had hit him with a sledgehammer. I know what that star meant to you, Gabrielle. It's a tough loss for you. And for me. Mary Kathleen's—"

Her lip trembled and she worked to gain control. "Yes," she whispered.

Her dad took the cardboard box from her slack hands, saying reluctantly, "You want me to pitch this in the trash?"

"No." Gabrielle carefully closed the lid and took back the box. "I can't do that. You couldn't, either."

"Sure doesn't seem right, but I don't know what else to do with all this glass." He let his hand linger against the burgundy box, stroking the smooth surface.

"It's not repairable, but I couldn't toss it out with the garbage. Holding it earlier tonight, I thought for a moment I felt Mama brushing her hand against mine.''

"Aw, honey." Milo bumped his forehead against hers as he gripped her hand. His eyes, like hers, were moist.

"Maybe I'll find a pretty jar and put the splinters and fragments in it. Turn it into a piece of modern art. What do you think?'' Clutching the box, she reached for another tissue.

"Whatever you want to do, honey, is fine with me. We can't change what happened, so if that's your attempt to make lemonade, go for it.''

She rattled the box and listened to the flat, scratching sound of broken glass, the *ping* gone forever. "I'll clean up the kitchen and put the food away after everyone leaves. You're going to take Nettie home?'' Opening the drawer near the front door, she tucked the box inside. Packages of Cletis's treats were squashed around it.

"She came in a taxi. All right with you if I chauffeur her back to her place?'' Unsaid, but acknowledged now, the fact that her dad should have prepared her for Nettie Drew.

"Sure, Pa.'' She kissed him on the cheek. "I think that would be a great idea.''

"Might take a while. She lives on the island.''

"Party on, Pa. I'm not going to wallow in melancholy.'' She swallowed the last of her tears and pitched the tissue in the trash. "Don't worry about me. I suppose I should warn you not to stay out too late and remind you to check the gas before you leave, right?''

"Mouthy brat.'' He hugged her. "You're my own special star, Gabrielle Marie, always.''

At his words, her eyes welled up abruptly, but she opened them wide so that tears wouldn't fall. No more tears tonight, at least not in front of her dad. If she had any tears left, she would save them for later, when she was alone.

With Joe and Oliver's departure, the party lost energy.

Shortly, people began filing out the door to choruses of "Great party, Milo" and "Good to have you home again, Gabrielle."

"Merry Christmas, everyone," she said brightly, waving farewell. "Thanks for coming." With every farewell, she thought of Oliver's face as the star had slipped through his childish hands, thought of Joe's posture, so fierce and protective as he'd held Oliver, and she thought, too, of Oliver and Joe, alone, in the sterile atmosphere of their hotel room.

And with every farewell, she heard her mother's voice.

Outside at midnight, saying her final goodbyes, Gabrielle lingered on the front porch, listening to the distant, deep chiming of church bells.

She'd forgotten this part of Christmas.

The scents, the flavors. The bells, that great, peaceful rolling-out of a sound that seemed to come from heaven itself.

Every night at midnight from December first through New Year's Eve, the church would ring its bells. How could she have forgotten this gift of Christmas?

Gabrielle stayed until the last sonorous gong died away, leaving the night quiet and serene under distant stars, real stars, not crystal symbols.

She stood for a long time in the silence with her face tipped up to those stars, letting the night seep into her and calm the storm of unhappiness inside her.

In that still, quiet sparkle of star shine, she knew that somewhere, in this universe or some other space and time, her mother's spirit watched over her.

Returning to the house, she grabbed a garbage bag and began collecting the debris from the party. In the living room, her dad and Nettie sat on the couch, talking, their faces serious. Nettie's shoulders angled toward Milo's, and his left arm lay along the back of the couch, millimeters away from Nettie.

"May I help you, Gabrielle?" Nettie rose.

"No, but thanks. There's not a lot left to clean up in the

kitchen. I cleaned as I went. Once I find room in the fridge for the leftovers, I'll call it a night."

"Four hands can carry faster than two." Nettie followed her into the dining room and picked up two platters.

"Six are better." Milo grabbed the empty jambalaya pot. "The three of us can make short work of this mess. Good thing you sent some leftovers home with Moon, honey. Think they'll last until morning?"

"Doubt it."

"Me, too. Moon's fairly passionate about his food."

Scraping salvageable leftovers into plastic bags and containers, Gabrielle moved swiftly from counter to sink and back as her dad and Nettie brought in the rest of the serving dishes.

Gabrielle, her mother and Milo had worked together after the tree-decorating parties as long as Gabrielle could remember, the cleanup sometimes more fun than the festivities.

She expected pangs of memories, that soreness around her heart to return, but the moments with her dad and Nettie were peculiarly comforting. Different, a reminder of loss, but— comforting.

Milo disappeared, saying he had to see a man about a dog, but Nettie remained, wiping the counters and table.

With the dishrag in her hand, Nettie faced Gabrielle. "I'm so sorry you were caught off guard. I wish Milo had told you that he and I are—"

"Dating?"

"I suppose that's the word. I can't think of a better one, but *dating* is not a word I'm comfortable with, not at my age." Behind Nettie's stylish, silver-rimmed glasses, her uncertain eyes met Gabrielle's. "I wish Milo had explained things first. So that you weren't surprised. That wasn't fair to you."

"Nor to you," Gabrielle admitted, grateful that the tightness around her heart had disappeared. Nettie Drew didn't deserve a cold shoulder from Milo's daughter. She was a good woman. Cultured, sensitive. *Nice.* Joe was right. "Pa didn't know how to tell me. So he avoided facing the issue, and it was too late. You were here." She took the dishrag, rinsed it and draped it over the spigot. Pressing it against the stainless steel, she said, "I have to admit I was—surprised. Maybe hurt, a little. Not your fault," she said, waving Nettie silent. "It was difficult at first, but Pa's happy around you. His happiness is important to me."

"That's very generous of you." Nettie rubbed her hands along the edge of the counter hesitantly. "But I realize how—how terribly awkward this situation has to be for you." Her index fingertips met in the center of the counter.

Gabrielle smiled and, reaching out, gave the woman a hug. "As strange as it seems for my dad to be *dating,* I'm getting used to the idea. Give me time, that's all."

"Time." Thoughtfully, Nettie took off her glasses and clipped the stems together. She held the glasses for a moment before saying, "You're a lovely girl, Gabrielle. Mary Kathleen must have been so proud of you. I'm sorry I didn't know her. Milo loved your mother immensely. He still does." Her smile was rueful. "I'm not Mary Kathleen, and I don't want to take her place with your father. I couldn't."

"Pa's lonely, Nettie. I'm glad he met you." Gabrielle meant every word. She would find a way to handle the emptiness inside herself, this forlorn voice that cried out for someone to *need* her. "This is hard to say, but I understand he needs more in his life than a grown-up daughter. A daughter isn't enough. You see, I decided he needed me, and I made decisions that affected him without listening carefully to what he was saying. I didn't really give him a chance to tell me about you."

Nettie reached out, and her glasses bumped Gabrielle's wrist. "But you haven't said what *you* need, Gabrielle. Did you see yourself taking care of Milo forever? Living here, letting your youth vanish year by year? Your intentions were admirable." Concern crumpled her face. "But in the long run, would your plan have been good for you? Or, ultimately, for

Milo? No one welcomes becoming the altar of someone else's martyrdom."

"Is that what I was doing?"

"I don't know. But your father might have believed that." Nettie tapped her wrist gently. "You wouldn't have wanted him to think that. I don't imagine you saw yourself as a martyr."

"No, I only wanted to help."

"It's been my observation, Gabrielle, that sometimes the best way to help someone is to step back and let him help himself. Or herself." She unfolded the stems of her glasses and slid them over her ears and back into place. Behind the lenses, her bright blue eyes were shrewd and compassionate.

"Were you a counselor, Nettie?" Gabrielle opened the refrigerator and moved the mayonnaise jar and a bottle of wine to make room for the last container of jambalaya.

"Oh, I still am. Part-time, though, but I love what I do. And work keeps my brain functioning. That and Ginkoba." Her smile was self-mocking. "But I hope what I said didn't come across as interference. Or giving advice where none was sought?"

"No." Gabrielle leaned her forehead against the refrigerator. Had her dad seen her actions as martyrdom, as taking away his independence? Lifting her head, she smiled brightly in spite of the lump in her throat. "I'm glad we had a chance to talk, to get to know each other a bit."

"Me, too. I like you, Gabrielle. Milo is very special to me. I think we both want him to be happy. But your happiness is equally as important to Milo." She looked around the kitchen. "Is there anything else I can do before your father drives me home? No?" She gave Gabrielle a hug and a light kiss on the cheek. "Good night. Thank you for your kindness to a stranger who came uninvited into your life."

"You're easy to be kind to, Nettie."

"Thank you, Gabrielle." Hesitantly, Nettie moved a plate

of fudge, frosted with green-and-red flowers, back and forth. "What do you know about Joe Carpenter?"

Astonished by the question, Gabrielle could only stare at her. Nettie had been on her way out the kitchen door, yet she'd stayed around to ask this completely out-of-the-blue question. "He moved here in high school, but he left before his senior year was over. I never heard why, though. He had a—reputation as a troublemaker, but I thought a lot of that reputation depended on smoke and mirrors. People talking and spreading gossip, but no one having the facts. That's about it. Why?"

Nettie's gaze was direct, the blue eyes piercing. "Because I think he's a man who hasn't had much kindness in his life. He stands on the edge of a group and watches, like a stranger. An outsider. He interests me. He and that boy of his. I like them both."

"So do I," Gabrielle whispered.

"Good." Nettie nodded as if something Gabrielle had said answered some unasked question. "Well." She paused. "And, Gabrielle, don't worry about your father. Good night again." And she was gone, the faint scent of lemony flowers remaining behind her, floating in on the cool air from the front of the house.

Nettie Drew left more than her scent behind—she left her friendship.

Outside, the low rumble of a car engine being started broke the stillness of the midnight hour. Milo, taking Nettie home.

As Gabrielle wiped the stove down and emptied the dishwasher, she considered Nettie's astonishing comments. An interesting woman, to spot Joe's stranger-in-a-strange-land aura so quickly.

Joe had never seemed at home in Bayou Bend.

Equally astonishing that he'd chosen to return here to raise his son.

Pushing her way through the kitchen door into the darkened hall, she headed toward the living room to check on the tree lights before going upstairs to bed. She walked through the hushed house, the glow of the Christmas lights pulling her forward, magic even without the star.

In the dim glow, she saw two figures and stopped suddenly, not entering the room. After starting the car, her dad had come back in to get Nettie. They stood close together in the archway between the living room and the front hall.

They were under the kissing bough Moon had hung there, their bodies forming one silhouette, moving together even as she watched.

The baggy sag of her dad's pants was that of an old man. But the passion in his embrace was that of a young man, vital, intense. It was the tenderness in his voice, though, that held Gabrielle motionless.

"Ah, Nettie, sweetheart," he said, the shadows shifting, moving as Gabrielle watched. "You make me want to wake up in the morning. You fill my life with sunshine. So much darkness. And now you. With me."

"Milo, Milo," Nettie murmured, her arms slipping around his neck to hold him closer. "You're my treasure, the best, best thing in my life. Ever."

Quietly, scarcely breathing, Gabrielle backed out of the hall into the kitchen, her heart drumming in her chest.

Letting the kitchen door swing silently closed behind her and making no noise, she dipped out a cup of the still-warm glogg. Sinking into one of the kitchen chairs, she dragged another closer. Lifting her feet onto the second chair and leaning her head back, she wiggled her toes luxuriously and stared at the ceiling.

Thoughts and feelings moved through her like a river current, lapping here, there, at her consciousness.

An exhaustion beyond the physical drained her of her last ounce of energy or will. She tasted the spicy glogg, breathed in its warm vapors.

As she sipped, she let her mind wander, let the events of

the evening swirl around, sort themselves out. Looked for the flow.

All in all, what a strange, unsettling night it had been.

Nettie and Milo.

Oliver.

Joe, the town's bad boy with a chip on his shoulder and attitude to burn.

Joe Carpenter, a man with a polished edge and a wary toughness lurking in the depths of his teasing brown eyes, a man who could make her heart pound like wild surf in a storm.

A man with a son who broke her heart.

Chapter Seven

"Daddy!" Oliver streaked to Joe and glommed onto his leg.

"Hey there, squirt. Missed you."

"Me one, me too." Oliver rubbed his face against Joe's jeans. "I have to finish my cookie." He trotted back to the O'Sheas' kitchen table, and Joe followed, one hand on his son's flour-stiff hair, relief flooding him.

Earlier, he'd been reluctant to leave Oliver, but, pinch-faced and withdrawn, Oliver had insisted he wanted to see Cletis and make cookies. Even if he did have to stay with Gabrielle.

"Gabby's one of the good guys, Oliver."

"Maybe. Maybe not. But I'll stay. Cletis wants to see me," Oliver had said, sighing heavily. "So I gotta go."

But the boy had stayed at the screen door, pressing his face against the mesh, Cletis on his feet. As Joe drove away, his son's reflection remained in the car's side mirror until the end of the driveway curved and Oliver was out of sight.

Now, obviously Gabby had worked some kind of magic on Oliver in the meantime, and Joe was grateful. Nothing he'd said last night as he tucked Oliver into bed had helped. Whatever Gabby had said to the boy or done with him today had worked, and Joe felt an enormous load lift from his spirits.

As he entered the kitchen, she looked up, arrested in the middle of plopping a spoonful of manila-colored dough onto a cookie sheet.

"Nice makeup, sweet pea." Joe traced the line of white flour down her cheek, over her chin and to the curved neck of her sleeveless dark green T-shirt. Streaks of flour decorated her faded navy shorts, collected in the cuffs. "In a Kabuki mood today?" Her skin was soft, yielding under the dusting of flour. "Hmm. What's this?" He touched his fingertip to a sparkly grain and licked. "Sweet. Sugar."

"Me?" Gabby batted his hand away.

"You? Nah." He licked his finger again. "The sugar, of course. What did you think I meant?" He had meant her, of course, the taste of her sugared skin lingering in his mouth. He should have resisted that tiny indulgence. But he hadn't expected the taste of her skin under the sweetness of the sugar. He'd meant only to tease, but the joke had turned on him, leaving him with a hunger sugar wouldn't begin to satisfy.

Shining brilliantly through the open windows, the sun washed the planks of the floor with gold, chased shadows into the far corners.

On a day like this, small indulgences could be forgiven, he decided, because some hungers were destined to go unfed. That was okay. He'd plotted his course. He could live with his decisions.

At least in the warm sunshine of Gabby's kitchen, he could.

Loneliness hit harder in the cold night, though. Made it harder for a man to remember what he knew he had to do.

"Me and Gabby made cookies." Oliver held up a heavily frosted sugar cookie tree. Colored sprinkles dotted the floor and crunched under his sneakers as he bounced up and down. "Here, Daddy. I made this one special for you."

"Delicious." Joe choked down the thick cookie. Actually, underneath the six feet of icing and decorations, the cookie was good. If you wanted to commit suicide by sugar, that is. He lifted Oliver into his arms. Sugary hands planted themselves on each side of his face, and Oliver smacked a kiss on his cheek. "How was the morning?"

"'Kay." Oliver settled against his hip.

"'Kay," Gabby said, half a beat behind Oliver. Lingering at the table, she rested one bare, tanned foot on the rung of the chair beside her. Her pink toenails and feet sparkled with sugar bits. "We melted crayons and ironed paper over them. Christmas wrapping paper," she explained seriously. "For presents. Oliver and I were doing a Martha Stewart day." Gabby held up a waxy purple-and-pink piece of tissue paper. Gold glitter poured off it onto the floor.

"Festive." One of the purple blobs looked a lot like a Christmas tree.

"We thought so. Right?" She laid the paper off to the side, away from flour and sugar but near Oliver and Joe.

"Yeah." Leaning forward in Joe's arms, Oliver swooped to the floor and smashed his hand against the glitter. He brushed his hands clean over the tissue with a happy sigh. "There."

"We baked half a million cookies, and we kept Cletis off the counter," Gabrielle added.

"Mostly," Oliver confided in a whisper to Joe. "But not always. And I gave him munchies. Lots."

"Cletis throw up much?" Joe nudged the collapsed fur heap under the table with his foot.

"Once or twice." Flour puffed in a cloud as she dropped a scoop back into a container. "We coped."

"I'll bet." Joe liked the way the sunlight gilded her skin and touched the hair along her temples with gold. "Milo and I ate lunch."

She paused, the rolling pin in her hand, as if she was about to ask him about their conversation. Instead, she said, "Coffee? Lunch? Gee, you guys know how to make a day-long feast." Rolling pin and flour container in hand, she danced by him, her topknot of hair flopping with each step. "Wild men. Layabouts." Dusting her hands over the sink, she said sternly, "We, however, have worked all day like dogs and have not eaten. Oliver and I expect high-class cuisine for our efforts, right, sweetie?"

Oliver nodded. "Def'nitely."

Joe smiled. At some point Oliver had picked up Gabby's *definitely* and made it his own.

He squirmed, and Joe swung him down to the floor. Circling Joe's thigh with an arm, Oliver leaned against him companionably, saying, "Hamburgers. Apple pie. Milk shakes. High-class—stuff."

"Where's Pa?" Gabby asked, making another round trip from sink to table and back. Opening the oven door, she shoved in the dough-spotted aluminum sheet and set a timer. "Did he come home with you?"

"He said he had errands."

"Nettie."

"That would be my guess. He took off like a bat out of—"

"A cave?" Gabby's smile melted over him like hot fudge, beguiling and seductive and completely unselfconscious.

"Yeah. I saw him slicking back a strand of hair to cover that kind-of-thin spot at the top of his head, so I figured he was off to see the lovely Nettie. Since he was so interested in his appearance."

"Mean, Joe." Gabby slapped him on the arm. "Pa prides himself on his manly mane. What if your hair started thinning?"

"I'd buy a whole new collection of baseball caps. Or I'd do the Michael Jordan look." He mashed his hair back with both hands. "What do you think?"

"If you could slam dunk, it might work for you, but, gee,

Joe, it's not quite you." She wrinkled her nose. "Good luck. I hope you inherited good, hairy genes."

"Hairy jeans?" Oliver covered his mouth and hooted. "You'd have to get your jeans cut and your hair cut and you'd have to shampoo your jeans. That's silly, Gabby."

Strolling to the sink with the last of the containers, Gabby laughed and thumped him cordially on the head. "Show some respect, youngster, for those of us one step away from Medicare."

Oliver's solemn eyes searched her face. "You're old, but not as old as Milo. Are you?"

Joe sputtered, Gabby laughed.

"No, sweetie, not as old as my dad, thank you very much."

"I didn't think so. Milo's *very* old, older than anybody."

"Oh, if Pa could hear little pictures speaking." Turning on the water, she said, "Of course, it would kill his image of himself. And, speaking of Pa, he's interested in Nettie." Not looking at Joe, she asked, "Did you know? Did Moon or Milo tell you?"

"About Nettie?" Joe had picked up the vibrations from the two and found the idea of Milo and Nettie rather touching. A winter love, a Christmas love between two people who hadn't expected passion to enter their lives again and had, unexpectedly, found each other. "No, Gabby, neither Moon nor Milo said anything to me about Nettie."

"Doesn't matter. I saw them last night. Milo and Nettie. Mistletoe. Kissing."

"I get the picture."

"Probably not, Joe." Her expression as she scrubbed her hands under the running water was contemplative. "It was quite—touching."

"You okay with it, sweet pea? Senior citizen romance?"

"I think I am. But, let me tell you, there was nothing senior citizenish about them, Joe." Her voice turned wistful. "I stayed awake a long time last night, thinking."

"Me, too. Not that all that brain-straining did me any good," he muttered, watching the silvery spray of water and the movement of her hands under it, reminded once again of his resolution that seemed to last only as long as he wasn't around Gabby. "How about you?"

"I believe I have some things sorted out. Maybe." She turned off the faucet and lifted her dripping arms up. Water slid in a glistening rivulet down the inner sides of her arms and she shivered. "Life's full of curve balls, isn't it?"

With Oliver clamped onto his leg, Joe followed her to the sink, handed her a paper towel. "Want to go Christmas shopping?"

"Me?" She turned so suddenly that his hand slid along her hip, settled against her fanny, the linen fabric of her shorts nubby against his touch.

He wanted to cup the sweet, slight curve of her hip where it sloped into her rear, draw her up against him, thigh to thigh.

Stepping back abruptly, he bumped into Oliver. Joe cleared his throat. He thought he'd settled that argument between his libido and his brain during the late-night hours after he and Oliver had returned to the hotel. Looked like that had only been round three of what apparently was going to be a hell-raiser of a battle.

Gabby followed him. "You're inviting me to lunch?"

"Hey, I can recognize a hint when I hear one."

"I'll remember that you can take a hint. In case I ever need that information." Again that slow, soft smile.

She was flirting with him. He caught that hint, too. They had agreed flirting was okay. But that was before his hormones and his good sense had struggled to the death. He and Gabby could be friends.

But no matter what he and Gabby had decided, Joe knew friends couldn't flirt. And last night he'd made that brutally plain to that feisty maverick romping through his blood and hog-tying his conscience and reason.

As he kept stepping back, she kept following, and Joe felt a line of sweat build up along his hairline.

Sweet, innocent Gabby couldn't realize what she was doing to him.

"Come on, squirt, let's get you out of harm's way." Lifting Oliver again, using his son as a shield between a shorts-clad, bare-legged Gabby who made his mouth water, Joe answered, "Sure. Lunch. You. Me. Squirt, here. Payback for a morning spent kid-sitting, okay?" Friends needed to pay back favors. Everything equal, balanced. That was how friendship worked, especially if he was going to make this man-woman friendship work with Gabby. "Lunch at some fine dining establishment with arches and fries."

"And hamburgers." Oliver leaned over backward, his head not far from the floor. "I love hamburgers and fries and cola and pie and—"

"Sure this child isn't related to Moon?" Gabby giggled and caught Oliver's arms as he swung them in mad circles.

That, of course, was the sixty-four-thousand-dollar question. Did Joe really want to know who Oliver was related to? And would it matter if he left that question unanswered?

To Oliver?

To himself?

What if, as he suspected, Oliver wasn't his son, not by birth, anyway. What if Jana had merely put Joe's name on the birth certificate for convenience, or for some perverse reason of her own?

If she had been that cruel, how would her decision alter his and Oliver's lives? Because it would. Wheels within wheels, but he'd die before he'd let any more hurt come to this boy.

As the silence lengthened, Gabby glanced at him, puzzled. "You know, Joe. Moon and his voracious appetite for anything animal, vegetable or even mineral?"

"Yeah. I'd forgotten about Moon's primary passion in life." Joe swung Oliver upright. The kid was like a rubber monkey, bending and contorting his small frame in Joe's arms. "You that hungry, guy? Hungry as old Moon man?"

"More hungry, a gazillion times more hungry," chanted an upside-down-again Oliver.

"That's that. We're going on an adventure." Whirling out of the room, Gabby left them.

Joe scarcely had time to wipe Oliver's face and hands before she reappeared. Some kind of pin scooped her hair back on one side. Every time she moved, the bells on the pin jingled. Slim stretchy black pants shaped her thighs and calves. He liked the snowflake cutouts sprinkled on the red sweatshirt hanging past her hips. When she bent over to slip into her shoes, the sweatshirt rode up and treated him to the sight of Gabby's very tidily curved rear end. Stretchy black pants might turn out to be his favorite female fashion.

In the gap between her black shoes and pants, white reindeer pranced across the ankles of her black socks. The lead reindeer sported a shiny red nose. Gabby was literally throwing herself head over heels into the spirit of the season. He gestured ankleward. "St. Patrick's Day socks, too?"

"And Halloween and Valentine's Day."

"I'm speechless."

"I noticed," she said dryly. "What's wrong with celebrating? I like holidays. I like celebrating." Slinging a black purse embroidered with three elf angels over her shoulder, she said, "Who's driving?"

"Since I can all too easily picture your car with a miniature Santa Claus and reindeer leaping across your dashboard, I'll drive."

"When did you become so conservative, Joe Carpenter?" She fluffed her hair free of the neck of her sweatshirt.

"Guess I'm not into the season the way you are. If it doesn't move, I swear you'd put a bow on it."

"Golly, until you brought the idea up, though, I hadn't

thought about the car," she mused. "Maybe I'll put a wreath on the front bumper. What do you think, Oliver?"

"Cool," he breathed.

Joe figured Oliver would be insisting on a wreath and dash decorations before the day was over.

An hour later in the washroom at Bayou Bend's local hamburger palace, Oliver hitched up his pants. "Guess what else I did today?"

Joe helped him cram his shirt inside his jeans and buckle up. "Damned if I know. Made a Santa Claus hat for Cletis?"

"Cletis would not like that. He would feel silly."

"Yeah, well, I can understand that. Wash your hands, squirt."

"I don't see handles." Oliver rested his chin on the side of the sink.

"Stand here. Right in front of this round circle in the wall. It's a sensor. To turn the water on and off."

"Cool." Standing on tiptoe, Oliver stuck his hands under the spray of water, moving back and forth as the water stopped and started.

"That's enough. We don't want Florida to turn into a desert." Joe took the rough brown paper and dried Oliver's obediently outthrust hands. "So you didn't make Santa Claus hats. What did you make?"

Oliver bent at the waist to peer under the stalls. Seeing no one, he whispered, "A present. For Gabby and Milo and Cletis."

"Did Gabby help?"

"No. It's a surprise. But she will like it," Oliver confided as Joe pushed the door open and they exited. "You can't tell Gabby I made a present. Christmas is for secrets. And this is a bi-i-ig secret." He stretched his arms as far out as they would go. "Promise?"

"I promise." Joe wondered what glitter-sprinkled, flour-dusted creation his son had come up with. "You're feeling better, squirt? About last night? And about me going off with Milo this morning?''

"Def'nitely."

"Because I wouldn't have left you at Gabby's if you hadn't been okay with it."

"'Course not." Oliver trotted by his side back to the wrapper-strewn table where Gabby waited for them. "Now I want to go into the ball cage. You come with me. Gabby, too," he offered.

Gabrielle watched the Carpenter men approach her. Joe's head was bent toward his son, Oliver's face was uplifted to his father. Joe had slowed his long stride to match the boy's hop, skip and jump. Joe's oatmeal beige, long-sleeved shirt was folded at the cuffs, and water spots marked the front. Hard to be a *GQ* guy with a six-year-old.

Interesting that the jeans-clad, leather-jacketed Joe had become this man in conservative, expensive clothes. She recognized the cut and fit of expensive tailoring when she saw it, and Joe's slacks and shirt made her long to touch their beautiful fabric, see how it felt against her skin.

Clothes like that made a woman think about the man beneath them.

But long ago, she'd dreamed about Joe in his leather jacket and tight jeans, too.

Joe and Oliver both looked at her as they stood beside the table, their expressions so similar she almost laughed. "That was fast."

"Unlike the females of our species, men don't take a lot of time lollygagging. We're efficient." Joe didn't look down at Oliver, who'd clamped his hands over his mouth.

"Ah. Getting even with me for my layabout accusation, are you?" She wadded up wrappers and stuck them on the tray. "Plus leaving cleanup duty for me. You don't think that's carrying revenge too far?" She dumped the tray's contents into a nearby bin, then placed the tray on top.

"Revenge?" Joe opened his eyes wide and looked innocently down at Oliver, who was hopping from foot to foot, his hands still clamped over his mouth. "Would two gentlemen like us be interested in revenge?"

"Yeah!" Oliver exploded. "But *you* was the layabout, not me. I worked."

"Go play in the ball cage, squirt. You've betrayed me. I'm crushed. Where's the loyalty these days?"

Oliver hooked onto Joe's hand.

"And gentlemen would help clean up." Gabrielle handed Joe a cardboard pie container. "Pitch it, buster."

He did. "Gosh, I sure do like a bossy woman. Something mighty appealing about a woman who knows her own mind. Makes a man start to fantasize—"

"Hush up." That dratted red flushed her skin again with his sly look, and she swatted him with her purse.

"I hear and obey."

"Right," she muttered under her breath. "Like I'd believe that."

He smoothed the wide strap of her purse where it had twisted over her shoulder. "Hey, I know my place."

She might have believed him if his touch hadn't lingered underneath the fabric strap, might have believed him if he hadn't been standing right within her space. She might have believed him if she hadn't seen the hunger flickering like eddies in the deep currents of his dark eyes.

Even with her inexperience, she recognized that expression.

Abruptly, breaking their linked gazes, Joe gave his son a slight nudge toward the tall wire cage before turning to her. "Coming? Or do you want to meet us later? Do some shopping?"

"I'll watch."

Bending down, he murmured, "You don't have to. You've earned your angel's wings for this morning." His breath slid against the curve of her ear and sent shivers down the length of her spine. "You and Cletis. I reckon we shouldn't leave him out." Laughter moved in his brown eyes as he watched her. Thin and elegant, his mouth lifted at one corner in amusement, and she wanted to smooth her fingers over the supple line of his upper lip.

"Oliver and Cletis have bonded. Cletis sold his loyalty for munchies. He follows Oliver around with this mournful, hopeful expression on his face and his tail in a question mark. But I think a winged Cletis would have as much chance of going airborne as a penguin would."

"That's an image that could give me nightmares. Cletis with wings and a halo." Holding Oliver with one hand, Joe placed his other hand against her waist, palm flat, just as he'd done the night before while guiding her through the throng of holiday-merrymakers.

And, exactly as before, her tummy fluttered, sensations curling through her, and her knees went slack. All these lovely feelings running riot in her blood, and she'd lived all her life without experiencing them before. Oh, a tingle every now and then, but nothing like this awareness of her skin, of her breasts, of every part of her. Like a parched flower, her body thirsted for his touch, for him.

But last night she'd understood the between-the-lines message, loudly and clearly. He'd said flirting didn't mean anything, not from his point of view, anyway.

Hard not to understand then that he was warning her off, letting her know he didn't mean anything with his teasing, sexually charged behavior, and so she'd fallen back on pride and zipped her own message back, her very own little devil making her say that Joe shouldn't expect anything from her, either—like sex.

She would have loved a photograph of his face when she'd tossed that into the conversation. She'd known that would stop his foolishly noble attempt to make sure she understood the difference between the town's very bad boy and its good girl.

Well, he'd changed during the last eleven years, and so had she.

Life could pass a woman by while she was waiting for it to begin.

Sometimes a woman had to know when she'd wasted enough time.

And maybe even reformed bad boys could learn a thing or two from a good girl who was looking to be a little bad.

With him.

Even good girls who weren't skilled at flirting could yearn to be naughty.

The idea intrigued her and slowed her steps. If Joe could rock her world with a touch, a look, not even trying, what would happen if she turned the tables on him?

A spark of mischief prompted her to slide her arm around his waist.

He stopped midstride, looked at her, frowning. "Gabby?"

A few yards ahead of them, Oliver shed socks and tennis shoes, tucking them into one of the cubbyholes in a row of blue shelves. With a determined look on his face, he climbed the two steps to the cage and silently pitched himself face first into the pool of multicolored balls.

"Yes, Joe?" She smiled brightly and held on for dear life, every nonaggressive cell in her body shrieking with terror. "What were you saying?"

"Nothing." Contemplating her, obviously thinking the situation through, he continued to frown. "Whoa," he said suddenly, pulling her out of the way of a careering tot chugging gaily forward. Joe's arm stayed, lightly, carelessly, though, around Gabrielle's shoulders.

"Thanks." That her voice was calm was an act of will and maturity, because her pulse skidded and leaped like grease on a hot skillet. Her body flushed from head to toe, and she stepped closer, again surprising a frown from him. She smiled.

"The barbarian hordes," she said, gesturing to the rampaging children swarming around them.

"Yeah. Uh, Gabby?"

"Yes, Joe?" She tipped her head back, brushed her hair off her cheek. Her silver angel earrings swung in a cool sweep along her jaw.

His frown creased a vee in his forehead, drawing his dark eyebrows together as he regarded her. He finally shrugged. "Nothing, I reckon." But his expression as he glanced away remained puzzled.

She liked this unexpected sense of power over him, liked the novelty of throwing him off balance.

Moth to the candle, exhilarated, she dipped and floated, aware with every second of the candle's heat, the danger. And with every passing second, her damnable curiosity urged her to hover ever closer to that bright flame, to see if it really burned as hot as it shone.

"Oops." She brushed her hand across the front of his shirt, scraped her fingernail near the pocket. "Ketchup," she explained as he jerked under her touch. "You'll have to soak the spot in cold water."

"Yeah." He watched her grimly.

"Or you could send it to the cleaners," she offered helpfully. His chest had been hard, the muscles tight to her touch.

"I could do that." He took a step back, propping himself against the edge of one of the round tables, and crossed his arms.

Something gleamed in his eyes, and Gabrielle caught the tail end of a second thought, hung on and stayed where she was. That gleam was pure, undiluted trouble.

"Send a lot of your stuff to the cleaners, do you, Joe?"

"That's what single guys do. Unless they have time to do their own laundry."

"You don't?" Keeping her distance, she let the conversation drift where it would while she collected her courage for another swoop toward the flame. "Have time?" Her tongue tangled over the simple syllables as his glance, intense and amused, speared her. "I mean, your job keeps you busy?"

"Milo asked the same question." A slight edge iced his voice. "About my livelihood."

"Right." She plucked at the hem of her sweatshirt, dug at one of the appliqués, trying to identify the exact moment he'd left the state of bewilderment and entered the county of back-in-control. She crossed her arms, aware with each movement of his gaze. Everything puckered to a delicious tightness and she shifted uncomfortably. "And what did you tell Pa?"

"That my job keeps me busy. That I've taken time off to be with Oliver." He leaned forward, cupped her chin and lifted it. "And, sweet pea, if you're interested, I work for myself."

"Oh. That's—nice." She'd never thought of the chin as an erogenous zone. Not until this moment, at least. "What kind of work is that, Joe?"

"I started a computer hacker company."

"Hacking's illegal. Isn't it?"

A slight, unexpected hostility replaced the amusement in his face. "You checking me out, too, Gabby? Like Milo?"

"What do you mean?" Gabrielle tried to see beneath the edginess. Like an old wound, pain was still there in Joe Carpenter, a pain she'd never understood, still didn't. Whatever the burdens of the past were, they needed to be put down. "You thought Pa wanted to check up on you?"

"Milo had legitimate questions. I answered them."

"And because he wanted to visit with you, you saw it as an interrogation? Pa's a lawyer. Asking questions is as natural to him as—as *breathing*. It's not personal. It's not interrogation, for heaven's sake."

"But isn't that what Bayou Bend would expect? That I'd be mixed up in something illegal? Something shady? Isn't that what everyone would predict for Hank Carpenter's troublemaking son?'' His mouth a tight line, he angled for a better view of Oliver.

"So you advise companies on how to keep hackers out of their systems?''

"Bingo, sweet pea. Got it in one.''

"Well, why didn't you say so at the beginning? So when did you start this company?'' Exasperated, she scowled at him. She was missing something. "I mean, asking someone about his business is not the equivalent of taking a deposition, even from Pa.''

His shrug was tense, controlled. "But I doubt anyone but you would opt for that interpretation right off. I suspect most everyone else would expect me to be breaking into computers. Or heisting them. And for anyone who's interested, I started my business six years ago, and it's been successful. Any other questions?''

Distressed by the shadow of bitterness that moved over him, she smoothed her hand down his arm. The emotion emanating from him swamped her and made everything else unimportant. "Joe, I don't know what drove you away from this town. Over and over you tell me that Bayou Bend is where you want to raise your son, but I don't get it. Why would you come back here if you believe everyone mistrusts you and thinks the worst of you? You wouldn't put Oliver in that kind of situation, not if you truly believed that this town has turned its collective back on you. Something, *some* memory brought you back here. Nothing else makes sense to me.''

"What a good girl you are, Gabrielle. First Jana. Now me. You'd give the devil himself the benefit of the doubt, wouldn't you?'' His mouth twitched in a semblance of a smile, but there was no humor in it.

In front of them, solemnly leaping out of the pool of balls, Oliver waved to them, dived back under.

She gripped Joe's shirt, crumpling the smooth fabric in her fist. "Listen to me, Carpenter. I told you once before, but you didn't hear me. Or didn't listen. Contrary to whatever you think of me, I'm *not* naive. I'm not stupid."

"I never said you were stupid," he drawled, unfolding her fingers one by one. "Never believed you were, either."

"But you've locked onto this idiotic idea that I'm naive, and that being naive, I err when I look for a positive interpretation of an event, don't you?" Her sweetness was acid-etched.

"You're innocent as a fresh-hatched baby turtle, Gabby. No more ability to protect yourself against the evil and nastiness in the world than those poor baby hatchlings scrabbling for the safety of the ocean."

"Lovely image you have of me, Joe." Funny, too, because that's how she had pictured Jana for an instant, leaving her infant as unprotected as those fragile turtles. Well, Gabrielle didn't care one bit for Joe's vision of her as naive and child-like. "A real ego-booster that you see me as this fragile, 'barely one step away from a fainting couch,' pathetic, help-less little female who's too naive and innocent to be respon-sible for herself? That about cover it, bub?" She gave him a good shake for the sake of principle.

"Gabby, look, you haven't lived in the same world I have. All my life. You've been raised in a nice town with nice par-ents and nothing nasty lurking in the closets of your bedroom. If you saw monsters in the night, why, I expect both your parents tripped over themselves to get to you and shoo away the scaries."

"Yes, I've been lucky. I wouldn't deny it for all the money in the world. And maybe what you imply is true. If I hadn't had the kind of family that I did, well, maybe I'd see life through darker glasses. But maybe I wouldn't. Because life gives us choices." She wadded his shirt even tighter and jerked. "Smarter, more sophisticated to look for the hidden agenda? Is that how you choose to live? Because that's one of the choices, Carpenter. How we see the world around us.

Is that your view of the world? The one you want Oliver to pick up from you?"

Joe tightened his mouth, but she had his full attention.

"You want your son to think that everybody's an enemy? That every time you turn the corner, the first person you see will have a contract out on you? Is that your world view?" she repeated, shaking him hard, anger ripping through her that he could be so blind to all the goodness and kindness out there waiting for him if he'd only take a chance and come out from behind the wall he put between himself and everyone but Oliver. "Because it's not mine."

"I know it isn't, Gabrielle. And that's quite a speech. Are you thinking of taking up the pulpit?" His voice was gentle as he tucked a strand of her hair behind her ear.

"Don't you dare make fun of me." She glared at him. "You don't have the right. You haven't walked in my shoes. And because I haven't walked in yours, I'm willing to cut you some slack. Think you could do the same?"

"You're fiercely loyal, you *choose*—" his smile almost broke her heart "—to believe the best, even of me, and you see the world as rich with possibilities and happy endings."

"I know life isn't a fairy tale." Fury licked through her, singeing every nerve ending. How could he reduce her life to such a simplistic interpretation?

"Do you, sweet pea?"

She nodded so hard, her forehead slapped against his chest.

"See, I don't." As if he were comforting her, Joe continued stroking her hair, tidying up the strands that had flown wildly as she'd tried to make him see that life didn't have to be lived with suspicions and behind walls. "Because the only happy endings I've ever seen were in books and movies. Not in real life. Life experience has taught me that truth. And I'm a good student."

"This is what you'll teach Oliver, too, Joe." She trapped his wrists. "What a sad, lonely legacy to leave your son. Because that's the legacy he will carry with him long after you're gone.''

Joe's head turned toward the ball cage. His eyes narrowed as he watched Oliver bounce up and down, flop back under the balls, leap back up. All alone, Oliver bounced and dived, bounced. Dived.

Alone.

Once more that sharp pain sliced through Gabrielle. She couldn't fix Joe's problems, no matter how much she yearned to.

Only he could.

And if he didn't? Couldn't? If the past couldn't be forgotten, forgiven?

Ah, she thought, clasping his strong wrists, there would be the real tragedy.

Dimly, she grasped that his tragedy could become hers, too.

Chapter Eight

Gabrielle expected that the rest of the day would be ruined after her outburst. She should have known Joe wouldn't let the atmosphere remain supercharged with tension. That wasn't his way. Lightly, good-naturedly, keeping away from emotional deep waters, he stayed behind his mask of charm.

There were moments years ago when she'd glimpsed the bitterness and pain he usually kept hidden. She'd witnessed accidental ruptures in the facade he'd created.

Had that long-lost nineteen-year-old man, with his leather jacket and attitude, been only a facade, too? One she'd sensed but had never gotten to know because he kept everyone at arm's length with aggression and flippant sexuality?

Like Oliver, when she'd first met him, staking out territory, had Joe claimed his own domain over the years, a place where he felt safe? Easier to keep folks at arm's length than to risk rejection.

Easier to reject them first.

Putting yourself at risk was opening yourself to enormous pain.

At thirteen, when she'd first seen him, she'd sensed that, sensed the shadows in him, but at fifteen, on the cusp of understanding, she'd been overwhelmed by the pure, raw power of Joe Carpenter's masculinity. And then he'd disappeared, taking his shadows and mystery with him and leaving her with this sense of some other land faintly seen, a land that called to her in dreams, her arms outstretched in a futile search, the shores of that distant place receding with daylight and business.

Christmas was a time to step away from the shadows, to rejoice in the light and promise of the season. No matter what he said, Joe had returned to Bayou Bend to close a circle. He'd come home.

Like her, he'd come back in search of a missing piece at the core of himself. She'd arrived at a crossroads in her life. Because looking after her dad had seemed like an answer, she'd grabbed at the excuse. Joe's excuse had been Oliver's need for small-town values. She was determined to find out what Joe's own need was.

They shopped. They snacked again in the food court. They shopped. Finally, when she thought she'd fall in a heap, to heck with the shop-till-you-drop mantra, Oliver asked in a mumbled aside for her help picking out a present for Joe. Still keeping a cautious reserve, though, Oliver didn't take her hand.

"Will you help me? 'Cause daddy can't be with me. Or it won't be a secret."

"Do you need money?" she whispered, stooping down. "I can loan you some. You can pay the loan back by brushing and feeding Cletis."

"I have five dollars." Oliver unzipped the wallet hanging by a cord around his neck. "See?"

Peering inside, she inspected the wad of singles, coins and a picture with ragged edges. "That should be enough." She patted the wallet. "Zip up your money bag and tuck it back under your shirt. Nice picture," she added casually, standing up.

Oliver regarded her warily. "It's mine."

"Of course it is, sweetie. Maybe sometime you'll show it to me. I'd like to know who the baby is. You?"

"Maybe." Oliver snicked the plastic zipper shut.

She'd caught a quick impression of a pale-haired woman pushing a baby stroller. If the baby was Oliver, the woman most certainly was Jana. Even though Gabrielle doubted that he remembered his mother, the picture meant something to him. A treasure.

"Joe," she said, turning to him and tugging at the hem of her sweatshirt, "Oliver and I are going on a scouting mission. We have important business ahead of us. See you later."

Joe squatted beside Oliver, said something Gabrielle didn't hear and gave his son a hug. "Sure?"

"Yeah."

"All right, then. Meet y'all at the exit in an hour?"

Gabrielle nodded. She hoped Oliver would find what he wanted in an hour. From what she'd observed of him so far, he was very deliberate about his decisions. Which tree, what sprinkles to put on cookies—the boy thought situations through at his own pace. She didn't want to hurry him, not on this particular decision, so she said to Joe, "If we're not there, call me on the cell phone. There's a pay phone near the exit. That way you won't worry, and Oliver won't feel rushed. Shopping's serious business, in case you didn't know." She scribbled out the number on a paper napkin.

Joe gave Oliver a slow wink. "I might do some shopping of my own."

Oliver studied him and then said, "You don't have to get me any presents. Santa Claus will bring everything this year."

"Yeah. But since I kind of like you, maybe I want to give you a present, too. Your first present from me."

"You bought me my shoes." Oliver stuck out a foot. Clots

of cookie dough and dirt spotted the less-than-spanking-new white.

"That was a dad present. Not an under-the-tree present." Joe's palm curved over his son's head, lingered. "This will be a special present from me to you, because this is a special Christmas. We'll be spending it together. We've never done that before. We need to celebrate." Joe glanced at Gabrielle. "I've been told celebrations are important."

"'Kay." Oliver hopped forward, backward. "A present for under the tree. Cool."

The poignancy of Joe's efforts to make his son's world perfect moved Gabrielle to press her hand against Joe's chest, smooth out the wrinkles she'd put in his shirt. "So you did hear what I said. When I leaped up onto my soap box."

"I pay attention to everything you say, sweet pea. I listen closely to what you tell me, to the words you use. And to the ones you don't use." His tone was nonchalant, his body language relaxed, but the rueful sincerity in his slight smile moved her in a way none of his sexy teasing had. This admission was one more crack in his diligently guarded mask. A gift, in a way, to her. "As a result of listening to excellent advice, I decided my son needed an exceptional present."

"Big job you're taking on, trying to find that kind of present. Whole lot of pressure you're putting on yourself, cowboy. Good luck." Impulsively, she raised herself on her tiptoes and pressed a kiss against his cheek. "You're something special, Joe Carpenter."

His cheek was scratchy under her lips, and before she stepped away, he turned and met her mouth with his, briefly, a brush of lips, firm, sculpted, turning hers softer and more yielding than she'd intended, transforming a friendly kiss into something else.

If she'd been in a movie, she would have heard bells, swelling music.

What she heard was her own swift intake of air, the leap of

her heart as Joe's mouth covered hers. She heard the sound of Christmas sparkling through her with every beat of her wayward heart.

In the middle of a crowded mall, she heard magic.

Her legs trembled. Her heels snapped against the tile floor. She opened her eyes and stepped back. "Um. Oliver and I should, hmm—" Her brain went blank. Her mouth still felt the shape of Joe Carpenter's mouth against hers.

"Go shopping?" Nothing simple in the dark depths of his eyes this time as he spoke, only a swirl of confusion. He lifted a hand toward her, let it fall to his side. Frowned. "I'll, uh, see you. Later." He didn't move.

Neither did she.

Possibilities hummed, sang between them, and she felt for the first time in a very, very long while as though she saw through a glass clearly, saw what might be if a person acted with courage and faith.

"Come on, Oliver. Time's wasting." She remembered not to take his hand. If he wanted to take hers, he could. She wouldn't step into his space uninvited, though. "Ready, sweetie?"

"Yeah." He unwound himself from Joe and froghopped to Gabrielle's side. "And I want a present for Suzie. She'll think I've forgotten her. And Cletis." He stopped, wrinkled his nose. "What would Cletis like?"

"Food?" Joe laughed as she and Oliver turned in sync to him. "Sorry. But if it's the thought that counts, Cletis doesn't seem to think of anything else, does he?"

"You have a real streak of cruel, don't you, Joe?" Mock-scolding, Gabrielle waggled her finger at him.

"No, no. But think about Cletis." Snickering, Joe captured her finger, stilling it, and curled her hand into his. "What else does he yearn for?"

"I know what I'm getting him," Oliver said. "And it's not food. But he would like snacks..." he trailed off. "I'll get him two presents." He patted his wallet-on-a-string happily. "That's it."

"We'll see you when we see you." Not about to risk another swoop toward the candle that was Joe, Gabrielle ushered Oliver toward the melee of the mall. Her mouth still burned.

Only a kiss. Barely a kiss.

But, oh, what a kiss from the right man could do.

Oliver settled on a shiny red vinyl food mat for Cletis. And a big bag of munchies. He found a pad of sticky notes for Suzie. "Because she leaves notes on the cabinets, on the front door," Oliver told Gabrielle with amazement. "Everywhere. Suzie says it's good to be organized. These will help," he said, sighing with satisfaction.

He couldn't find a present for Joe. Nothing was special enough.

"Do you want to make your dad a present, sweetie?" Gabrielle asked finally when Oliver seemed on the verge of a total meltdown. They were seated on a bench outside Nature's Nest, where the display of colored liquids and rocks had drawn Oliver.

He swung his feet back and forth, clunking them on the inside of the bench. "Maybe."

"If you made him a present, did all the work yourself, you'd be giving him a part of you. Something that no one else could give him. And that would be the best present of all. I mean, I'm not a parent, but, gosh, Oliver, Pa still has ceramic pots and picture frames I made for him years ago. He wouldn't part with them for all the gold and diamonds in the whole world."

Oliver raised his head. His feet hung motionless. "Picture frames? You know how to make those?"

"Sure do." And if she couldn't remember exactly how, she'd make darned certain she had good instructions.

He fingered his wallet. "Maybe a picture frame, Gabby."

And then he smiled at her, a six-year-old killer smile that melted her.

She wanted to hug him.

She didn't.

Instead, folding her arms over her purse as she held it in her lap, she nodded thoughtfully. "Pictures are important. They're the past. A picture is a memory of a moment that will never come again."

"Like your star."

She sighed, but agreed. "Like the star, Oliver." She'd hoped that issue had been settled while they were baking cookies. Digging into her purse, she found a roll of Life Savers and offered it to him. "But I have the *memory* of the star, sweetie. I have pictures of it, from other Christmases. Those pictures are more precious to me now than ever. Pictures are memories frozen in time."

Her voice cracked a little at the end, and Oliver stretched out one chubby hand and patted her knee. "I have three pictures."

"Well, then, you understand."

He patted her knee again before retreating. "My daddy would like a picture in a frame."

"Want some help making one?"

For a moment she thought he might refuse.

"You could show me what colors and material you wanted, and we could spend a morning putting it together. If you're interested. You could wrap it and put the present under your own tree in your new home."

He slid off the bench and faced her. "A picture frame. Cletis can help, too."

She extended her hand to shake Oliver's, as close as she could come to a hug. "Done. We have a plan."

He shook her hand. "Def'nitely."

That easily, the problem was solved. Gabrielle felt as drained as if she'd run a marathon. Oliver's present for Joe had been a crucial decision. She wouldn't have left Oliver alone with that worry weighing down his narrow shoulders. Too important to leave to chance.

"We've done a good job shopping. But now I'm thirsty. Want a drink?"

Walking beside her, he shrugged. "'Kay." For an instant, she thought he would take her hand in his. He looked as if he would.

He didn't.

Surprised, she realized how much she wanted him to, though, wanted his trust more than she could have imagined wanting anything in the last year.

Like his father, the son had sneaked into her heart and made a place for himself.

When they returned to Joe and settled plans for supper, Gabrielle played up their shopping efforts, exaggerating for all she was worth. Putting the blarney on it, as her dad would say.

And with the memory of Joe's unexpected kiss still tingling on her lips, she flirted, moth once more to his candle, safe in the crowded mall and with Oliver an oblivious chaperon.

Close, close to the heat.

But safe.

Later, as they ate dinner in a family restaurant in the mall, she toyed with her earrings, fingering the smooth angel wings, her throat tipped up. Joe stopped abruptly, spaghetti strands dangling from his fork. He grinned across the table at her. "You're flirting with me, aren't you, sweet pea?"

"For a fellow with a reputation, it took you a long time to catch on." She dipped her chin and looked up at him through tangled lashes.

"Just checking, that's all." Meticulously, he twirled his fork in the spaghetti until all the strands were tightly looped around the tines. "Feeling pretty adventurous, aren't you?" Taking a bite, he gazed at her, his expression enigmatic, the planes of his face sharp and shadowy, mysterious in the dim light of the restaurant.

"Yeah," she said, mocking him with a grin of her own as she gave her earring one last flip and nudged his foot with hers. "Flirtin' like all get out."

"Careful, Gabby." His voice had a harshness she didn't recognize. Not anger. Not annoyance.

Something else.

Something enticingly dangerous.

The burred tightness pricked her curiosity, tempted her closer, moth wings fluttering.

She didn't want serious. She didn't want complicated. Not now. This was a day for exploration, for flirting, for trying out her wings.

She wanted to make Joe laugh, to chase away the shadows lurking in him.

And she wanted to see his son's killer smile again, that lighthearted, gap-toothed smile that would break hearts in ten years.

As his father's had.

Unlike his father, though, Oliver would have people in his life who cherished him, who would guide him through turbulence. Unlike Joe, Oliver wouldn't be labeled the town's bad boy.

It was late, the crescent moon shining silver in the dark sky, when Joe dropped her off at her house, Oliver's snores a faint whistle in the back of Joe's four-by-four.

Her father hadn't left a porch light on, and the house was dark. Either he had gone to bed, or he was still with Nettie. In the shadowy recesses of the porch, Joe placed one hand on either side of her face as she turned to him after unlocking the front door. The screen door wobbled against his hip. "Have you enjoyed flirting, sweet pea?" In the deep darkness, he was shadow in shadow, his voice lapping against her like an incoming tide.

Her back was pressed against the heavy wood of the front door. Her throat closed up, and for a moment she didn't think she could speak. "Yes." She moved restlessly, her feet scraping against the floorboards. "How about you?"

"Oh, yeah, Gabby. I enjoyed flirting with you. You've no idea how much." His voice turned thick and rough-edged.

She couldn't resist one last dart at the flame. "How much, Joe?" she whispered, sliding her arms around his waist.

At the skim of her arms around him, he moved his right hand, slid it through her hair. Her hair comb jingled and clattered to the porch, rolled silent. Lowering his head, he brushed his nose against hers, stroked it and waited. His breath, coffee-tinged and rich with the scent of him, stirred against her. She clenched her fists into her sweatshirt and fought the whimper of need rising, rising, from some deep, unknown place inside her.

Then, his movements slow and easy, molasses over warm pancakes, he took her mouth with his, fitting his mouth over hers and sealing their lips together. Over his shoulder, she saw the moon flicker into darkness as her eyelids drifted shut with the whimper that sighed from her to him.

His thighs nudged hers, and she stepped into the cradle of his body without even thinking, the urge to be close, closer, pulling her deeper into the mystery and wonder of his embrace. And with her movement, the kiss turned dark and hungry, urgent in a way her dreams had been.

Standing on tiptoe, she stretched herself against him, her breasts molding to the hardness of his chest, her thighs trembling against his, and she linked her arms around his neck, tugging him closer, the hunger in her leaping to meet the hunger she tasted in him.

This was what she had wanted, this merging of her self with someone else. No, she thought, dazed and lost in sensation as he curved his palm over her stomach, no, not *someone* else. Him. *His* touch, his lips. *Him*. Joe.

Since she was fifteen, this was the touch she'd waited for. No one else's.

This was the reason her curiosity hadn't tempted her since. Until now. Until Joe.

Her knees buckled, and she sagged against him, only the strength of his arms holding her upright as he moved forward, bracing her against the door as he bent, fitted their bodies tighter together, sealing them mouth to mouth, body to body.

Sliding both thumbs to her chin, he tipped her head back and kissed her throat, nipping at the base as his fingers stroked her cheeks and earlobes. "Joe," she said frantically, pulling him tighter. "*Joe.*"

"Me, Gabrielle. It's me you're kissing." He kissed her again, his tongue sweeping inside her mouth, calling her tongue out to play, and she surrendered to the moment, to the sensations she'd known in her dreams of him.

Behind her closed lids, she glimpsed the shimmer of that distant land, clouds parting around it, the sun gleaming on its green shores and blue water.

And then Joe rested his head against the door, his hands supporting him, his body taut against hers. His breath was as ragged as hers, his chest heaving. She felt the thunder of his pulse throughout her body, her own heart pounding wildly to the beat of his.

He lifted his head and took her face between his hands. "And that wasn't flirting. In case you wondered."

And then he was gone, the taillights of his car a wink of red in the night.

Two days later, oddly formal and distant, as if that moment on her porch had never happened, Joe handed her a folded white paper. "Oliver and I are inviting you, Milo and Moon to a tree-trimming party at our house. No glogg."

"Wise decision," she said, opening the piece of paper. A

waterfall of miniature plastic trees, stars and reindeer shimmered into her lap. "Oliver made this, I gather?"

Stretching his arms wide, Joe lay back on the blanket they'd spread on the pine needles at the beach park. "No, smarty britches, I did." Dappled with sun-and-pine shade, his smile was lazy. "Hidden talents."

She looked at the letters straggling across the page. Lots of red. Green. Lots and lots of glitter. She glanced up at the dock where her dad and Oliver were wetting their lines. The picnic had been Oliver and Milo's idea. She and Joe had retreated into this amiable formality as if they were strangers.

Or people who knew each other too well.

In front of her, the gulf was a brilliant blue, the warm December sun gold in the sky. She read the painstakingly printed words and folded the paper along its creases.

Joe must have helped him. Every word was spelled correctly, the erasure marks showing under the bright colors. She tucked the invitation into the basket she'd brought. They would have labored over the invitation a long time. She cleared her throat. "Sounds like fun. What can I bring?"

He reached up and twined a strand of her hair around one finger, drawing her closer, almost as if he couldn't help himself. "Oh, yourself. In a pair of socks I haven't seen."

"I can manage that."

"You have more?"

"One or two pairs left." She had a drawerful of seasonal socks. If pushed, she could wear a different pair for the whole month of December. "If I can't bring food, can I help cook, set up?"

"Nope. This is a guy project."

"Notice I didn't offer cleanup services."

"I noticed. Oliver and I have it all planned out. Pizza and cola. Beer and wine for the old folks." Joe stroked the end of her hair against her throat. "For your information, that's you and me, too. He's been determined to have a party ever since he was at your house. Incidentally, thanks for helping him with the last of his shopping. And wrapping. The presents are in a bag, waiting to be unveiled at the big moment."

"Christmas Eve?"

"Nah. The moment we put the tree in its stand. I think the squirt can hold out until then. Possibly. He takes them out of the sack, turns them over and over, and then puts them back in." Joe rolled over onto his stomach and braced himself on one arm. "Gabrielle, we need to talk."

"I'm sure we do." As if she were back on the porch with him, her body constricted, flushed, blood pooling fast in her tummy.

"I've been thinking about what you said the other day when we were talking about my job and why I came back here."

She blinked. Readjusted her thinking. "Umm. All right."

He plucked a pine needle from the blanket, bent it, sniffed. "You need to know some things about me."

His comment took her from hot to cold, that fast. That was the line people used when they had bad news to tell, catastrophes they wanted to prepare you for. "What I need to know about you, I already do." Scooting down, she faced him. The breeze off the water was chilly against her bare feet. Her sandals weighted down one corner of the blanket.

"You never asked Milo what we talked about the other day at breakfast, did you?"

"Even if I'd asked, he wouldn't have told me. Lawyers are good at keeping secrets. Pa's *very* good." Not looking at Joe, she traced the line of the root-bumpy ground. "Your secrets are your own, Joe."

Her sun-washed face was half hidden by her hair. He wished she would look at him. Telling her would be easier if he could see her clear, truthful eyes. Looking at him, though, she wouldn't be able to hide her revulsion, her disgust at what she heard, and there would be no chance to pretend that this fragile friendship they were building could continue.

He didn't want to lose her friendship.

While he wasn't clear what, exactly, he wanted from her, he knew he didn't want her walking out of his life.

Now, watching her trace the ground beneath the blanket, Joe almost reconsidered. He didn't have to reveal this ugliness to her, not on this beautiful golden day. There would be other days. A better time.

There would always be a better time.

And he would be a coward if he didn't let her into his life enough to trust her with this truth about himself.

If she walked away, that would be her decision.

Something inside him curled up protectively against the idea of Gabby's turning her back on him.

But at least he would have given her the information she needed to make her decision. She deserved the truth about him. Fair was fair, especially between friends.

Staring out at the blue, blue gulf, its purity mocking him, he began. "Once upon a time—"

Laughing, she brushed her hair away and turned to him. "I thought you didn't believe in fairy tales, Joe."

"This is a true story, sweet pea."

"Does it have a happy ending?"

"I don't know how it ends."

"A never-ending story, then." She studied the ground again.

He'd been wrong. Better, much better if she hadn't looked at him with those innocent eyes that hadn't seen the world he had. Too hard to strip away everything he'd built up and go back to that nineteen-year-old punk he'd been. Doggedly, he started over. "Once upon a time there was a boy. A stupid, reckless boy. An angry boy."

Softly on the afternoon air, her words came to him. "I think I knew this boy. A long time ago."

"Could be, Gabby." He rolled to a sitting position and faced the water, his profile to her. "He hated everyone."

"Did he, really?" She still lay beside him, facing away from the water. Her skirt draped in dark red folds against her bent leg.

"Yes, he really did. He hated himself, too, of course. Why wouldn't he? He had no reason to like who he was. No one else did. He was an outsider, on the fringes looking in the windows of other people's lives. All he wanted to do was smash his fist through—anything. Everything."

"Someone must have been concerned. For this angry boy." Lying flat, she dropped her head onto her arms.

"If you were writing this story, someone would have loved him. But not in this version."

"What happened to the angry boy?"

Joe heard Oliver's shriek of laughter as Milo whipped up his fishing pole and splashed water.

"He grew up."

"Did he stay angry?" Such gentleness in her husky voice, that he wanted to run, run as far away from her as he could before he had to finish the story.

He nodded slowly, remembering the anger that had lived with him. "The anger went underground, building like a pressure cooker inside him. Year by year. Until life taught him lessons he hadn't learned earlier. Until then he—"

"Was a troublemaker?" She stretched out her arm toward him, the sun glowing against her skin as she lay unmoving on the blanket, only her clear eyes watching him with understanding, an understanding that gave him courage to continue as she let her arm fall to the blanket. "A guy with an attitude?"

"You've heard this story?" He almost picked up her hand and covered it with his. But that would have been cheating.

"One like it." She sat up with a quick movement, her skirt flowing darkly red around her calves and thighs, like the crimson rush of the sun at the end of the day. "But in the one I know, the boy wasn't bad, not really. More a case of style and image, it seemed to me."

"Wrong story, sweet pea." He pleated the blanket between his fingers. "In this story, he was very bad. Oh, sure, he wasn't evil. Mixed-up, confused, no question. But, yes, he also did bad things."

In a movement so fast he wasn't prepared, she took his fists in her hands, forced them open. "Ever heard of forgiveness?"

"Sometimes a person can't forgive himself." He lifted her hands from his, placed them on the blanket, freed himself of the comfort of her nearness. "And that's what happened with this boy. He didn't mean to hurt anyone, but he was in the wrong place at, oh, I reckon you'd have to say it was the right time, and people got hurt."

"What did you do, Joe? You wouldn't have hurt anyone on purpose. Not you."

Watching his son, Joe rested his chin on his knees. "I hated my father. Over the years I've tried to understand him, and even now I can't. He was a mean drunk. He lied, he cheated, he stole. Nobody's candidate for Daddy of the Year. And he was fast with a fist. With me. With anyone who was in his way. Didn't matter. Fed up, my mom walked out on us when I was four, and I never heard from her again. Once my old man said she'd died. Years later I found a yellowed newspaper notice of her death. Said she was survived by three children. Daughters."

"Ah, Joe, Joe." Tears in the soft sound of his name.

He couldn't have borne her touch at this moment. Her pity would have unmanned him.

"She should have taken you with her. She should have, she should have." The sound of her tears was hushed, a counterpoint to the music of the breeze and water.

"It's only a story, sweet pea. And an old one at that. Nothing to fuss about."

He heard a sound from her, but he couldn't look at her. Not now. If he did, he'd never finish the damned story. She deserved to hear the rest of it, the worst.

A seagull flapped to a landing a few feet in front of them. Flinging the bits of torn-off bread high into the sky, Joe watched the circling white wings dip and soar, birds catching the bread airborne.

"Anyway, me and my old man moved every year or two, sometimes more often, keeping one step ahead of the bill collectors, the local sheriff. I never knew. By the time we landed belly-up in Bayou Bend, there must have been warrants out for my old man across half the country. I knew we wouldn't stay here. We never stayed anywhere. But I was tired of being that poor, snot-nosed Carpenter kid."

She stirred, and her bare feet flashed into his view, the toes shiny with alternating red-and-gold polish. "So you became Joe Carpenter, the boy who drove teachers crazy because he was so smart but never paid attention, the boy mothers warned their daughters to stay away from. And, of course, all the girls followed you around like bees after honey."

Even with his chest hurting with pain and regret, he smiled at her exasperation. "They weren't interested in me. They liked the thrill of being seen with the town's bad boy."

"You sell yourself short, Joe. I liked you. Other people did, too. Maybe you couldn't see that what drew people to you wasn't simply your 'cool' attitude, the lure of the forbidden. You made people laugh. And you charmed us all, Joe, one way or another." She was quiet, her sigh blending with the rising wind.

"The night I kissed you outside the country club was the night I left town."

"I remember."

He'd thought she did. All the sparks flying between them like fireflies that night at Moon's tree lot had been lit that crazy, sad night so long ago. "I left you and went home. My old man had boosted a car and stuck up a convenience store. Shoot, he didn't remember what he'd done. I saw the gun and the money and figured it out. For me that was the last straw.

I was so angry I couldn't think straight. All I knew was that I'd had enough of him, of his meanness and destruction."

"What did you do?" Her toes dug into the sand, their sparkle dusted with white.

"I wanted out, away from him. If he'd been awake, I don't know what I'd have done. Hit him back? Maybe. The anger was building in me like those volcanoes you see pictures of, everything collapsing and then spewing out and out, destroying everything in the way. Like a dope, I stuffed everything in the car and headed back to town, thinking I'd leave the car somewhere and everything would be all right."

"Oh, no. Why, Joe, why? That was so—"

"Stupid? Reckless?" He laughed, remembering the fury and the anger that had burned away reason. "Of course it was."

"What were you thinking? That you could keep your father out of jail?"

"Don't see good motives where they didn't exist, sweet pea. I wasn't protecting *him*—" the word was like acid in his mouth "—I didn't want one more scandal landing on top of me, one more reason for people to step off the sidewalk when I came walking down it. Town after town, move after move. The same. Settle in, try to put down roots, and then my old man would mess everything up. I'd see the pity in teachers' eyes, and I'd say something smart-mouthed, anything to erase that pity. And then the old man and I would skip town, start over. But the pity and the disgust always, always surfaced. Sooner or later. So I took the damned car and left. I didn't know where I'd dump it. Somewhere far away from Bayou Bend, that's for sure."

As he watched Milo and Oliver, Joe finally comprehended something. The words coming out slowly, as if he were only now sorting out the emotions of that damning night, he said, "Because I wanted to come back. Bayou Bend was beginning to feel like home, and I was tired of running. I never understood that until this minute. I thought I hated the town. I didn't."

"And that's why you came back after you'd run away?"

Joe held his hands out, palm up. "The two years I lived here were the longest time I lived anywhere."

"That's the reason you brought Oliver back here. This was home to you."

"Sure didn't seem that way at the time, not when I was flying down the highway at a hundred miles an hour. All I could think about was running away. Putting as much space between me and this town as I could. I couldn't get that old junker of a car to go as fast as I wanted to."

"You were stopped." She flung a chunk of bread skyward.

The flash of her slim arm was a curve in the reddening sunset. "I told you, this story is about a reckless, angry boy without a lick of good sense. No, I didn't stop when I saw the police in back of me. Two counties south of here, I crashed the car and, in a blind panic and rage, broke one cop's jaw and fought off the police until they cuffed me and hauled me to the station."

"The news never made the papers here. Why didn't any of us ever hear anything about it?"

From the corner of his eye, he saw her tightly folded, shaking hands. He believed he sensed her withdrawal from him. That, after all, was what he'd expected. "Because your daddy, Gabrielle, saved my soul."

"What?" In a whirl of dark red skirt, she jerked upright, facing him on her knees.

He looked for disgust in her face.

He saw bewilderment.

And something softened in her eyes as she steadily regarded him—acceptance, compassion, he didn't know what he saw, but in that moment, he knew he'd lay down his life for her.

For Oliver, because he was his son.

For her, for this woman who offered him friendship when he'd expected nothing.

Hoped for nothing.

Chapter Nine

Joe told her the rest. The humiliation a corrosive in his soul, he explained that Milo had persuaded the local police to reduce the charges, that Milo had put his own reputation on the line for Hank Carpenter's troublemaking brat, and that Joe had never understood why.

"Because Pa saw something good in you."

"If you'd seen him that night, you wouldn't think that. Your dad's eyes were the coldest, hardest eyes I'd ever seen in the face of any man, not even one whomping the living breath out of me. I called Milo because I didn't know any other lawyers. I didn't have anyone else to call."

"What about your dad?"

"If I'd been dying, sweet pea, I wouldn't have called him. Never. Not on this earth. Anyway, he was in an alcoholic stupor. A year later, cirrhosis of the liver finished what he couldn't accomplish on his own. Thus, my pappy played his last scam and avoided prison."

"I'm so sorry, Joe. I wish you knew how much. What a terrible burden for you." Her husky voice splintering, she reached out toward him once more, still on her knees in front of him, her skirt glowing against the darkening sand and pine needles.

Abruptly, awkwardly, he stood up, stuck his hands in his jeans pockets and paced back and forth, keeping his back to her, his gaze stretching to the horizon where the sun blazed in the darkening sky. "Because of your dad's intervention, I served six months, work-release time. I might have gotten off with probation without the resisting arrest charge, but Milo told me I needed to take responsibility for my own actions, regardless of what my father had done. I needed to get my life in order or I would wind up like my father, the way I was wasting my opportunities and talents."

"Never. You would never have turned out like your father." Her voice rang with a certainty that made his breath hitch in his chest.

All these years later, Joe couldn't believe that Milo had made everything so clear to him in the midst of all that turmoil and fear. "I was the one who'd gone off half-cocked. *I* was the one who hadn't thought the situation through. 'Consequences,' Milo said. 'Damages required reparation.'"

"That sounds like Pa."

"He was right, too, to take the hard road. I needed to step back and look at my life, get a handle on it, because at the rate I was going, I was headed nowhere good."

"You were young, Joe."

"Not that young. Truth to tell, I don't ever remember feeling *young,* not in the way you mean. No, I was responsible for what I did, and Milo helped me find a way through the darkness."

"How did Pa work his magic?" In back of her, red-gold water lapped at the shoreline in irregular curves.

"Oh, after he'd made it clear to me that he wasn't going to help me walk away scot-free, then Milo talked a blue streak, told the cops they had some discretion in how they reported the 'incident.'" Joe ran both hands through his hair, easing the ache in his head as the salt air blew over him, through him, a strange cleansing. "The 'incident,' Milo called it. Sheesh. The cops were licking their pencils to write up theft, robbery, traffic violations, resisting arrest, assault. I had visions of living the rest of my life *under* the jail. But in that calm, rational way he has, Milo kept saying the incident could be handled. Oh, he didn't try to excuse what I'd done, Gabby—"

"No, Pa's not into excuses. Face the music and learn from your mistakes." Bits of sand clung to her skirt as she rose and confronted him. In the failing light, her eyes were troubled. "I can't see him as being hard or cold, though."

"You weren't the one standing in front of him with your arms cuffed in back of you. He emphasized my stupidity, quite eloquently, in fact, but he said he knew me, could vouch for my essential character, and that the incident rose as much out of fear as stupidity."

"You *were* afraid, Joe. Of your father, of having your life collapse around you one more time. Pa understood that."

"Think so? He didn't know me. We hadn't spoken more than five words to each other before that night."

"Then why did you call him to act as your lawyer? What made you think of him? Why not let your fingers do the walking through the yellow pages?"

A gull shrieked in the red-gold sky. Streamers of pale clouds lay like whipped cream between the muted colors. He hadn't considered anyone but Milo. He knew Milo would come, no matter that he'd had to travel two counties down from Bayou Bend at ten o'clock at night. He'd known that as surely as he'd ever known anything in his life. Strange, now, thinking of that certainty.

"That summer your dad broke his leg—"

Her skirt frothing around her ankles like the incoming tide on the gold sand, she turned to him. "I remember. I'd turned fifteen and gone to camp for the month. I was looking forward to starting my sophomore year, being in high school, maybe getting to go to the Junior/Senior prom. Most of all, though—" she sighed "—I was excited about the chance to see you in the halls every day. From a distance, of course."

Her smile was rueful.

Doggedly he returned to his story. "Anyway, I saw your dad sitting on the porch with his leg in a cast and on a foot-stool. A few days in this humidity and heat and a yard can become a jungle. The lawn mower was sitting beside the car in the porte cochere, so I went over and fired up the mower. Never said a word. Mowed the yard, clipped bushes. Left. I showed up every week until I knew you were back."

"Pa told you I was home?" Her face was soft and puzzled, and he grasped that the complications of his life were so totally alien to her that she must feel as if she were listening to a story in a foreign language.

"No, sweet pea, I saw your itty-bitty bikini hanging on the clothesline in the backyard, so I didn't come back. And you know something? I pictured you in that scrap of cloth for the rest of that summer and into the fall. Pretty little Gabrielle in her bright pink bikini." Remembering, he started to touch her face, but didn't.

She blushed, a tide of her own suffusing her face as she ignored his comment and said, "That's how Pa knew you, then. You must have talked during those weeks, had an iced tea. He got to know you, what you were like. That's why he seemed so cold at the police station. He was worried for you. Worried *about* you. Don't you see?"

Joe thought back to those long, hot afternoons. The roar of the mower, the smell of the grass. Milo, sitting on the porch, watching through hooded eyes as Joe pushed through the heavy tangle of weeds and grass. "Gabrielle, your dad never said two words to me. I never spoke to him. Money was never discussed."

"Pa didn't pay you? That's strange. He's not cheap."

"I wasn't mowing his yard for the money."

"Why did you help, then? What did you want, if not

money? With your father's situation, you would have needed extra cash."

"I had a job in Calhoun's garage, fixing engines. I made out all right." Joe frowned, thinking hard, his original impulse lost in the intervening years. "Damned if I know why it seemed important to me to mow Milo O'Shea's yard that summer. I saw him. I started mowing. It seemed simple. No complications. Each Saturday afternoon, he left a thermos of tea by the mower. That was that. We never talked. And you know something?" Stopping, Joe took a deep breath as the realization struck him. "Those hot, sweat-drenched afternoons were the happiest times I'd ever known. Your dad. Me. Nobody talking. Nobody yelling. Everything *simple*. Just a normal summer afternoon mowing the yard. A Beaver Cleaver afternoon. Funny, huh?"

"Not so funny, I think." She touched him then, and he jerked away.

He couldn't let himself accept her sympathy. Sympathy was another form of pity. Whatever he wanted from her, and he was becoming increasingly confused about that, pity was nowhere on the list. "Anyway, Gabrielle, the police found the spark plug my father used to break in the car window. My old man hadn't taken it out of his pants pocket. Splinters of glass in the cuffs of his pants matched up, so it was obvious he was the one who'd heisted the car. Nobody placed me at the scene. The clerk at the store indicated that the old guy was the single robber involved, the tapes from the outside surveillance camera at the store corroborated his account, and your dad made counseling part of the deal. Because I hadn't been drinking, there was some flexibility possible despite the fighting. My juvie escapades were sealed, so the cops agreed to the arrangement. Milo put up bail, took me to your house, fed me. That's how I knew about his cooking. He fixed red-eye gravy and biscuits. Best meal I'd ever had."

"I didn't get home from the after-prom dinner and parties until daybreak. I can't believe I didn't see any signs that anyone had been at the house. Mama must not have known about it, either.''

''She didn't. Milo said she'd gone to the hospital to stay with a friend.''

''I remember now. The Potter baby was ill. Mama didn't want Anna Potter to be alone.'' Frowning, she shrugged. ''I'd forgotten.''

''I didn't ask Milo to keep the incident secret—'' he laughed ''—I started calling it that, too, but to the best of my knowledge, Milo never told anyone about that night. Moon knows. I reckon one of his cousins down around Sarasota picked up rumors. I don't think Moon ever told anyone, either. The way he likes to talk, I'm surprised he kept his mouth shut. Would have been a swell piece of gossip to pass around.''

''Moon wouldn't. He talks, but he's careful about not hurting people. A lot of big, tough guys are like that. All that strength makes them careful about using it against other people. Joe—'' she laid her hand lightly on his arm, stopping him as he walked to the blanket ''—what did Pa want to talk about the other morning?''

Looking down at the curl of her hand against him, Joe wished he were a different man, a man who could turn to this woman and— What? Offer her himself? A man like him with a woman like Gabrielle O'Shea? His darkness to the sunshine of her innocence and hopefulness? She deserved better.

Hard, though, at Christmas, not to think of what-ifs.

''Will you tell me about your talk with Pa?'' she repeated softly.

''Sure. Milo asked me about my work. About Oliver. I answered. Small talk, nothing more.'' But Joe hadn't told Milo everything about the boy who, no matter what, was his son. ''Milo offered to take Oliver fishing today, we shook hands and that was that.''

''Nothing about that night?''

''Not a word.''

Her hand tightened. "He wants you to know what happened in the past isn't important, Joe. Believe me. Let it go."

"Yeah. I suppose. The past shapes you, though, makes you who you are. You're sweetness and light." He lifted her hand from him as carefully as if it would break.

"And what are you, Joe? Because you're no longer that angry, confused nineteen-year-old boy."

Breaking free of her grip, Joe squatted to grab the edge of the blanket and shake the sand out of it. "I'm an unexpected father, Gabrielle."

"So you are." Stooping, her feet sinking into the sand, she lifted the other end of the blanket.

Joe glanced briefly at her solemn face as he handed her sandals to her. "With a son who desperately needs me. I'm all he has."

"Will you be enough, Joe?" Gentle, the words. Sharp, the sting.

"I don't know what you mean."

"Think about it," she advised, slipping into her sandals. Not looking at him, her face sun-flushed, she collected paper plates and cups, tidying up.

Her point eluded him.

The day was over. He'd done what he had to do. He'd told Gabrielle the worst about himself. What happened next would be entirely up to her.

He would have to live with whatever she decided.

And if she decided never to see him again?

It would be the smartest decision she could make. He had too many dark corners in his life, too many rough edges for someone like her to waste time on.

As for him, hell, he hadn't come back to Bayou Bend expecting anything. He'd already gotten more than he'd dreamed of. He could see a future now, for him and Oliver in this town. And if that picture of the two of them seemed incomplete, lonely, so be it.

Until Oliver, he'd been alone all his life.

As Gabby held one end of the blanket, Joe cracked the blanket hard. Sand gritted against his face.

Now his job was to protect Oliver. His biggest debt was to this boy. Step by step, Joe intended to pay his debts to the past. Birth son or not, Oliver was his, problems and all. He couldn't imagine a woman taking on that kind of uncertainty.

A clean slate.

He drew the air deep into his lungs. With his debts paid, a man could endure loneliness.

Matching blanket ends with Gabby, he halted, a thought snapping through his confusion. "Gabrielle, I think I know now the real reason I had to come back to Bayou Bend."

"Why's that, Joe?"

"To make the past whole. To fix it. Like Milo said, for reparation. I guess I felt I owed something here. Maybe to Milo. I don't know. I haven't figured everything out."

Her hand brushed his as she took the blanket from him. "Maybe you owed something to that boy who ran away."

For a long moment, he stood, her hand next to his, Gabrielle watching him steadily, her breasts moving gently up and down with her slow breathing. Stunned, he couldn't move. The moment acquired a clarity that stunned him. "Maybe," he said finally.

Sticking two fingers in his mouth, he gave a shrill whistle. "Hey, Oliver! Milo! Time to haul in the lines." Bait bucket in hand, Oliver trotted toward him, suntanned and grinning, Milo by his side.

Joe felt his heart constrict with emotion. *This* was his future. This child he'd sworn to make a life for, to provide the home Joe had never had with his own father. Strolling toward the dock, he waited for Oliver to reach him.

Thoughtfully, Gabrielle finished folding the blanket.

She'd accused Joe of being noble once before, thinking he was trying to let her down lightly. In her own insecurity and shyness, she'd missed too many clues. The man was too darned noble for his own good. He wouldn't see an elephant in front of his face if it bellowed at him.

So intent on explaining to her all the sins of the past, he couldn't see the forest for all the trees. Way she saw it, and she guessed Milo did, too, was that Joe Carpenter had been more sinned against than he'd sinned. Of course Joe didn't see that.

The ride across the bridge back to the mainland was quiet. One arm crooked on the door where the open window allowed the salt-and-flower-scented air to blow in, Joe didn't say anything. Weariness deepened the lines around his eyes, but each time he glanced at her, she believed she saw a peace in him that she'd never seen, the wariness gone, replaced by this acceptance.

From the back, Milo and Oliver's occasional comments mingled with the hiss of the tires on the road and the hum of the engine, lulling her to sleep. Her last conscious thought was a drowsy awareness that the four of them, together, felt good. Right, in some indefinable way. Nice, the four of them.

A family. The words drifted in as if spoken aloud. *Family.* On the sound of the word, Gabrielle slid into sleep.

The next two weeks collapsed on themselves with plans for Christmas. Bonded by their fishing expedition, Milo and Oliver went clamming, crabbing and fishing again. One crab, released. One bucket of coquinas, dug up from the sand. Mesmerized by the way the minute creatures in their iridescent shells dug themselves back under the sand, Oliver wanted to cart them home. Milo told him they would die away from the gulf, so Oliver upended the blue plastic bucket. "He was so fast, I had coquinas squirtin' through my toes, honey," Milo told her later. "The kid's got a good heart."

Joe and Oliver included Nettie in their tree-trimming party, and that felt right, too.

Walking into the hall of Joe's new home, Gabrielle was speechless. The wide staircase was looped awkwardly with ropes of pine branches; Christmas lights of every size and shape twinkled around doorways; and in the living room, the tree— "Oh, my lord," she gasped, seeing the tree again, "it's—"

"Beautiful," Oliver said happily.

With every step anyone took, the tree merrily shed needles. Straight in its stand, it rose majestically toward the ten-foot ceilings. Lights curled, drooped, swooped around it. Popcorn strands wrapped it like a package.

"Beautiful," Gabrielle agreed, with a lump in her throat. It was the perfect ugly tree. Beautiful in its transformation, its top, like that of the O'Shea tree, was bare.

"I broke your star, so it's not fair for me to have a star on my tree when you don't got one," Oliver informed her with a melancholy sigh. "Next year, me and daddy will have a star."

But it was the house that turned her quiet as Joe gave her the tour, showing her the renovation projects he and Oliver had already begun.

Joe had plans for his house.

Rooms empty of furniture and knickknacks were filled with plans, with possibilities. Permanence.

"See the grain of the wood under this cracked varnish, Gabrielle? It's beautiful oak. Think how it will look when I've sanded and refinished it."

"Big job." She ran her hand over the crazed-and-blackened varnish of the banister. "Who are you going to hire to do a project of this size?"

"Me." Chest stuck out like a Thanksgiving turkey's, Oliver pushed past her. "Me and my daddy are strong, and we are going to ren..ren..." He turned to Joe for help.

"Renovate," Joe said, and love rippled like a current in his voice as he spoke to his son. "We're going to—"

"Work like *dawgs* and paint and scrape and get dirty," Oliver explained in a whirl of words. "We are going to do all the work ourselves. Me. Daddy. We don't need nobody else."

Moving back to the living room, Joe ripped open the new

boxes of ornaments, handing a box to each person while Oliver unwrapped the ornaments her dad, Nettie, Moon and she had brought as tree gifts.

"I like this one." Oliver hung a ceramic crab on a branch at eye level. The branch bent toward the floor under the weight of the ornament. "Yeah," he said, moving back, "this is my favorite 'cause me and Milo went crabbing. But we didn't bring any home."

Gabrielle gave Oliver a tiny cat bell with wings and a halo. She thought it was a sign of progress that he didn't hang the ornament at the back of the tree. And when he thought she wasn't looking, she saw him stroke the cat's whiskery face gently, each stroke setting the bell to chiming.

She smiled. Oliver's feelings toward her were confused, mixed, sometimes hostile, sometimes friendly, but he was beginning to permit her into his world. In fits and starts, granted, but she figured nothing worthwhile was built in a day. Or week.

As she turned to hang another ornament, her eyes met Joe's. Pensively, he returned her gaze, almost as if he were trying to understand something, and as their gazes held, the room seemed to narrow, dim, until the two of them were left in candlelight and silence.

But he didn't say anything, nor did she, and the moment passed.

Later, Moon, Nettie, her dad and Oliver made a foray to the kitchen, looking for more pizza.

"Like what we've done with the place, sweet pea?" In the candlelight of the living room, Joe's eyes were serious, a question in them that went beyond the one he asked.

Pizza slice in one hand, wineglass in the other, and her mouth filled with cheese, Gabrielle nodded.

She grasped that the house was a symbol for Joe and for Oliver.

Joe had bought an old house when he could have bought one of the newer houses on stilts, one of the fancier houses in the new subdivisions that sprang up overnight in old pine forests and timberland. Stripping the growth down to the sandy soil and bulldozing ancient trees, the developers marched across the land, leaving concrete footprints and noise where there had been green trees and quiet.

Joe was making a home for Oliver, but Joe was making a home for himself, too. Watching the two of them tug at the balustrades and discuss what they were going to strip first, she wanted to weep for both of them.

She decided wine made her too sentimental.

Or maybe it was the pizza.

Shaking off the seriousness, she headed for the CD player, looking for music. Placing her wineglass on the shelf beside the system, she brushed her hands down her bronze velvet slacks and flipped through cassettes, records and CDs before saying, "We need music. Any requests?"

She recognized the presence at her back without turning around. In the corner of the candlelit room, shadows offered privacy as he lifted her hair with one hand and bent down to her neck, to the shallow indentation at the base of her skull. The kiss he placed there sent shivers down her spine, and she shuddered. His kiss was one quick, delicious prickling of her skin, and then he let her hair fall.

His finger stayed against the spot he'd kissed, a substitute for his lips. "Merry Christmas, Gabrielle," he whispered, and turned back to the others gathered around the tree.

After the tree-trimming party, as one day turned into the next, she felt on the verge of some momentous discovery.

Dropping Oliver off or picking him up, Joe lingered with her over coffee, eggnog and, one especially warm day, iced tea on the porch. Long silences punctuated their talk. She told him about her house-sitting company, how she'd gotten started. He explained that after his probation ended, he'd joined the army and learned about computers, deciding eventually to start his own business.

And in the words and silences between them, something

quivered, like a thin, fragile green stalk struggling through the darkness toward the sun, something that could bloom or be blasted by a sudden frost.

Keeping a careful distance, Joe flirted with her. She flirted back, sensing that they were walking carefully among emotional minefields, as if the wrong word, the wrong look, would trigger...*something*.

Clinging to Joe, to Milo, Oliver continued to keep the distance he'd established between himself and Gabrielle. No matter how carefully she approached him, he kept her at arms's length, frowning once when he saw Joe lean over her and cup her neck with a hand. Stepping back, freeing herself of Joe's light grasp, Gabrielle met Oliver's scowling, terrified eyes.

Moon invited all of them to crew on his boat during the annual Christmas Boat Parade.

"Do we gotta wear a costume?" Oliver asked hopefully.

"Damned straight you do," Moon answered. "Anything you want."

Moon's expression, where utter delight mixed with chagrin that he hadn't thought of the idea first, made Gabrielle laugh, a quickly smothered cough. No one had ever worn costumes, but Oliver had tapped into Moon's love of the theatrical. She wouldn't be surprised if Moon coerced the rest of the parade participants into costumes now that Oliver had presented the idea.

Gabrielle loved the boat parade. All the magic and mystery of the season were spun out over the cool darkness, night and river shimmering in an enchantment of color.

As far back as she could remember, every year on December 21, regardless of when the date fell, regardless of the weather, Bayou Bend boat owners decorated their boats, no matter what size or type, with strings of lights, turning the boats into floating displays of sound and sparkle against the dark water of the bayou. The boats would leave the creeks and bayou and head toward the wide bend of the river where it flowed through the center of town, boats drifting by in breathtaking beauty to the music of watchers along the way who sang carols back to the passing boats.

The parade ended at the luminaria-lined docks, where candles flickered in sand-weighted bags. As each boat arrived at the town center, it would turn off its lights, leaving nothing more than the golden glow of the luminaria in the darkness. One by one, the silent boats would slip into darkness, disappearing until only the lights of the final boat shone bravely on the river.

The crowd would grow quiet as the lights on the last boat winked out.

For a moment, joined in silent darkness, there would be a sense of community, of humankind, whatever the religion, joined together against the blackness of hate and anger and fear.

And then, at a signal from the lead boat, all the boat lights would come back on, blindingly, fiercely triumphant against the darkness. A sigh, as if everyone had been holding their breath, would rise up from the crowd, join the cheers and laughter and light.

Oh, she loved the parade of boats through the bayous and creeks, joining in a grand stream through the center of town. She loved the jostle and bustle of her neighbors, the wonder of that moment of darkness yielding to light.

In the depths of her soul, she was reminded in that moment of the fragility of life, of earth's majesty spinning through the darkness of eternity and space.

Sometimes the blaze of light moved her to tears.

Oliver allowed her to help him with his costume. Gabrielle knew better than to suggest an elf or angel costume. Wavering between a seal and a robot, he finally decided with Milo's help that he would be a red crab. Red for Christmas. "A crab, 'cause we're going on the water and I will be Sandy Claws."

The idea worked for Gabrielle. "Okay. But Pa has to help us with the padding for the crab's body."

"My daddy will make my claws. They will be sharp and scary."

Milo helped. Joe made the claws. Not sharp, but sufficiently scary to satisfy Oliver's bloodthirstiness. Gabrielle found red leggings and worked with Oliver to make a crab head.

Days later, costumes ready, the boat decorated, they headed to the bayou.

"Can't be Sandy Claws without a Santa hat," Moon offered, plopping his own hat on top of Oliver's headpiece as Joe swung Oliver aboard Moon's boat.

In a splash of red and pink, the sun melted into the creek water. A fish erupted from the water, twisting and turning in a gleam of shining scales, startling Oliver. He squealed with delight. Setting Oliver on deck, Joe reached back to Gabrielle to give her a hand on board.

"Hey, you forgot. I grew up around water." Gabrielle rolled up the bottoms of her jeans and took two steps back, preparing to launch herself forward.

"I like the socks, sweet pea." Joe closed her in his arms as she came flying over the gap between dock and boat. "The Santa seagulls are kind of cute, I have to admit. Gives us a theme for Moon's boat."

With Joe's arms tight around her and her body plastered against him like white on rice, she couldn't think of a comeback, not with his heart pounding like a snare drum against her own, and her breath caught somewhere south of her rib cage.

But Oliver looked toward them, his Santa hat drooping over one eye, and she smiled, took a shuddering breath, stepped away from the sound of Joe's heart calling her, and said, "C'mere, sweetie. Let's get your life jacket on you. You can take it off once you're on dry land again."

With everyone in life jackets and at their assigned stations, they set sail, catching the evening breeze. White against the blaze of sky, the sails flapped and filled with air in a great whoosh, moving back upriver toward town.

Earlier in the day, Moon and Joe had sailed the boat from its berth upriver down into Mosquito Creek, from which point they would start and join up with the other boats as their turn came to swing into the parade lineup.

While Moon and Joe moved the boat to its starting point, Milo and Oliver had followed in the car so Moon and Joe would have a ride home and back again after an early supper.

Left at home, Gabrielle had mock-complained that she was stuck once more with scullery duty. Nobody had paid any attention to her.

She hadn't really wanted them to.

She'd had Christmas plans of her own to complete in the early afternoon, and she didn't want anyone around while she set them in motion. Everybody deserved surprises at Christmas, and she'd finally decided what to give Joe.

Now, watching Oliver leap from one end of Moon's boat to the other, Gabrielle felt her heart leap with him, taking sail into the night.

The accident happened shortly after Moon slipped into line, about thirty boats back from the first one. Ahead of them, Gabrielle saw the shine and twinkle of electric reindeer and Santas. Tiny Italian lights outlined sails and spars. Some boats were outlined from bow to stern and up to the top of their sails. Smaller putt-putt boats were turned into water floats for elaborate figures shaped out of a myriad of lights. The chug of engines was muted by the hum of voices singing along the banks of the creek and river.

Entranced, Oliver stayed beside Joe near the bow of the boat. Gabrielle was halfway back on the port side, her life jacket bunching up her sweatshirt uncomfortably with each movement. Reaching for the buckle on her life jacket, she saw Oliver catch a glimpse of the boat behind them, saw his astonishment at the moving illuminations that moved from bow to stern, port to starboard. Joe had turned to catch the bowline Moon pitched his way.

One arm outstretched, Joe didn't see that slight shadow dart away toward the stern.

As Oliver bolted past on the starboard side of the boat, Gabrielle began moving, some instinct sending her into motion before she realized what she was doing. Her boat shoes gripped the deck as she ran flat out toward Oliver. "Joe," she called, her voice catching in the wind.

He turned in her direction.

Not quite at the stern, Oliver leaned over the side of the boat for a better look, his small rear end rising skyward.

Gabrielle vaulted over the anchor and grabbed. Her fingers scrabbled against the slick fabric of his life jacket as he disappeared into the water. Ripping off her jacket, she dug one foot into the railing, balanced herself and dived deep, stroking furiously as she plunged into the chilly water.

The last thing she saw was one crab claw flailing in the water. Downstream, Oliver's Santa hat floated, moved by the wake of the passing boat.

Oliver was nowhere in view.

"Damn, Moon, stop the damn boat!" Joe's frantic shout carried to Gabrielle as she pulled and kicked in the direction of the hat, terror lending her strength.

The darkness enveloped her, salt and brackish water filling her nose. She would later think how odd it was that she couldn't hear a sound, couldn't see anything except the waterlogged Santa hat. Somewhere a small boy with two claws had to be bobbing alone, safe in his life jacket.

Oliver had to be safe.

Why couldn't she see him? Had he hit his head on the boat as he pitched forward? Was he trapped underneath one of the boats? Anything was possible.

She inhaled, kicked hard and dived deep, searching in the blackness for movement, for the sight of a small, helpless boy. As she came up for air, thrusting against the water, her lungs burning, she flung her hair out of her way and trod water for an instant, scanning the water's surface for any movement, anything.

There, fifteen feet downstream and off to her side, she thought she saw a head. Kicking across the river's current, she stroked toward the pin dot that had to be a head.

Afterward, she would wonder why her throat was sore. When she heard nothing but silence around her, everyone else had heard her screaming Oliver's name with every stroke she took.

As she closed in on the dot, stroke by stroke, pulling with every ounce of energy so that she could intercept it, the dot bobbed, grew larger, turned into Oliver's head, his eyes wide and amazed as he floated serenely along.

"Hey, Gabby," he sputtered through a mouthful of water as she caught him in her arms and used her feet to keep them in one spot until Moon and Joe could turn the boat around. "This is neat, but I'm getting cold. Can we go back to the boat now?"

"You bet, sweetie." Sobs shook her as she rested her chin against his wet head. "Anything you want."

Holding the small, squirming boy tightly to her, Gabrielle swallowed her sobs. As Moon's boat circled near them and Joe reached out for both Oliver and her, she knew what was most important in her life.

With no warning, no clue, she'd fallen in love with Joe and his stubborn, terrified, wary son. She wanted them both in her life.

And she wanted to be part of their lives. She wanted to strip varnish and make Halloween costumes and wake up each morning to the sound of Joe's breath in her ear, to the snuffling snores of Oliver down the hall.

Chapter Ten

Joe grabbed Oliver from Gabby's arms and thrust him toward Nettie, reaching down again for Gabby, a bedraggled, stringy-haired Gabby, who at that moment was the most beautiful woman he'd ever seen. Retching creek water, she hung over the side for a moment before regaining her balance as Moon swung his boat clear of an oncoming motorboat.

"Oliver?" she gasped, clasping her cold hands on Joe's arms, her eyes smoky rings in her pale face.

"Oliver's fine. He thinks he's had an extra adventure. We need to get both of you dry." Her teeth chattered and her body shook against him. Or his shook against hers. He wasn't sure. All he knew was the sheer screaming panic that had taken him as he saw Oliver and then Gabby fall into darkness. "Come on, sweet pea, you're solid ice. Moon's going to turn the boat around and head back to the car." Trying to warm her, he rubbed her arms hard and turned to Nettie.

Nettie had brought towels. "I like to be prepared," she'd murmured. "Even for midnight swims."

Gabby went belowdecks to see if she could find something

for herself and Oliver to wear. Oliver didn't want to leave the flotilla of illuminated boats.

After the scare they'd all had, nobody had the heart to deny him this treat. Joe sure couldn't. The kid was a trouper, for damned sure. Clutching Oliver close, Joe clenched his teeth.

If he hadn't, he would have howled like a wounded dog, a terror he'd never known forcing its way up from his gut. Oliver. Gabby. He could have lost his son. Could have lost her.

Keeping his mouth clamped shut, Joe took Nettie's towel and wrapped it around Oliver, drying him off and stripping his crab costume off in soggy, heavy clumps.

Without the life jacket, Oliver would have drowned. He couldn't swim, and in the heavy costume he would have sunk like a stone to the bottom. Gabby wouldn't have seen him. It was a miracle she'd seen him, anyway, that small dot almost invisible in the noise and confusion.

As long as he lived, he would never forget the sight of her, her slim, sweatshirt-weighted figure cutting through the water, spotlights blinding her, her hair flat against her skull as she'd reached Oliver and held him so that they could see he was safe.

She'd given him his son back.

Moon's sweatshirt dangled around Gabby's ankles, but it was warm and dry. Gabby found a belt to tie around the waist of the sweatshirt she gave to Joe for Oliver. Even belted, the shirt dragged along the deck, but it didn't matter, because Joe had no intention of letting Oliver out of his arms.

He kept one arm around his son, the other around the woman who'd saved him, and each breath was labored, the knot of terror under his rib cage painfully constricting his breathing.

They wound up being the last boat in the parade, but Moon knew what to do, and he played the scene for all the drama he could wring from it, taking a bow as all the lights came back on.

Joe couldn't let anyone else hold Oliver. His arms had frozen around his son. And somewhere in the miracle of darkness and light as they floated toward the dock, he sent a silent thank you to Jana, for the gift she'd given him in spite of everything.

It no longer mattered to him why she'd put his name on the birth certificate, he no longer cared that she might have played him for a fool. As he breathed his thank you, he forgave her. Whatever had driven her no longer mattered.

It was in the past.

Whatever Oliver wanted to know about his mother, Joe would tell him, and he would give Jana the benefit of the doubt as Gabby had suggested.

With Oliver safe in his arms, and Gabby, wet and shivering, by his side, the pain he'd lived with all his life was suddenly set free, a balloon floating up and away in the dark.

Oliver fell asleep on the way home, his stiff hair scratching Joe's cheek.

Once he'd tucked Oliver into bed, creek-smell and all, Joe went to the shower. For a long time he stood under water so hot it stung his skin, tears streaming down his face and mixing with soap and water as he leaned his forehead against the steamy tiles and cried for the first time since he was five years old.

The next evening, Nettie and Milo asked Oliver to come for a B movie night. "Bad movies, the worse the better. And popcorn," he added. "We're planning on staying up until midnight. If you can stand to be with the old codgers, that is."

Joe hadn't wanted to let Oliver out of his sight. He did, though.

He had to, for Oliver's sake.

Alone in his own house, he sat in front of the tree, watching the lights twinkle and listening to the creaks and groans of the house.

The ring of the doorbell brought him out of his reverie, and somehow he wasn't surprised to find Gabby at his door. Shifting from foot to foot, she was clearly nervous. He'd never seen Gabby this fidgety. "Is everything all right on the home front?" He peered around her, half expecting to find Oliver.

"Umm. Yes. Everyone's fine."

"Good." He rested his hand on the door, suddenly ill at ease himself in the charged atmosphere.

"Are you going to invite me in, Joe?" She brushed a swath of hair back behind her ear and straightened her shoulders. "Because I'd like to come in."

"Sure," he said, puzzled. Gabby wasn't flirting, but the atmosphere was humming like an electrical field between them. "Come on in." He opened the door wider, and she stepped in sideways, not looking at him, her arms wrapped around her waist. "Can I get you something to drink? A glass of wine? Soda?" He shrugged. "Whatever you want, sweet pea."

At that, her head jerked up, and her eyes met his. "Good. That will make everything much easier." She squared her shoulders, looked around the hall. "Let's go to the living room, Joe."

"All right," he said slowly, intrigued by her determination and militant air. "The living room it is, then."

"Sit down, Joe. Please." With one hand, she pushed against his chest until he sat down on the couch.

Then she climbed into his lap and circled his neck with her arms. Her slight weight wriggled against his lap as she made herself comfortable. Resting her forehead on his, she tweaked the top button of his shirt free of its buttonhole, working her way steadily down to his waist. She took a deep breath and tugged his shirt free of his jeans.

He covered her hand with his. "What are you doing, Gabrielle?"

"Golly, Joe, I'd expect a man of your experience to know what I'm doing."

The lights were dim in the room, and he couldn't see her face clearly, but he thought she smiled. "Maybe you ought to spell it out for me. I've already had one glass of wine."

Her small, capable hands were tugging at his shirt and smoothing the skin of his chest, tugging at the tendrils of his chest hair until he couldn't think clearly. "That's good, Joe," she said earnestly. "Because this is a celebration."

"Is it?" Without even thinking, he twined his fingers in her hair, stroked the angle of her chin. "You're confusing me, Gabby."

She slipped her arms under his shirt and around to his back, tracing his ribs with her clever fingers. He shuddered.

"You like that, don't you, Joe?" she asked in a husky whisper that made him shiver again.

"Uh, yeah, sweet pea, I really do." He stood up, taking her with him and then reversing their positions until she was curled on the sofa and he was standing. And then he took a good look at her.

She was wearing some red, slinky outfit that clung and curved to her. High-necked and long-sleeved, the dress shifted and moved with her. He could swear he saw the outline of her panties. He knew he saw the small pooch of her nipples. Gabby wasn't wearing a bra. Joe blinked.

"Okay. I need an explanation. Fast."

"You're perspiring, Joe," she said sweetly, sliding her feet out of a pair of the highest heels he'd ever seen. Thin straps of shiny black, they thunked onto the floor.

"Damned right I am." He stuffed his shirt back into his jeans and scowled at her. "Does Milo know you're here?"

"Probably. Pa's not stupid." Curling her nyloned feet underneath her, she rose to her knees and slipped her index finger into the loop of his belt. And then she tugged, bringing him one step closer.

He hadn't expected that and he pitched forward, balancing himself with one hand against the couch.

"Ah, much better." She rose up and smoothed herself against him. "Yes. Definitely better."

Her kiss was sweet and innocent and hot, a need in the way she kissed him that almost shattered his good sense and his caution. He had just enough of both left to break her hold and take several giant steps away from her. Away from temptation and warmth.

"You don't know what you're doing, Gabrielle." He leaned against the window near the tree, trying to rein in the mad gallop of testosterone and lust. And that other emotion, too, the one he couldn't put a name to.

"Oh, Joe, you nincompoop. I know exactly what I'm doing. I'm seducing you. I'm propositioning you. I haven't waited this long not to know my own mind." She scrambled to her feet, her skirt inching up into the danger zone.

"That's very flattering, but believe me, you don't want to do that." He backed up flat against the cool glass as she moved in front of him, her stocking feet resting against his bare one. Her toes nudged his.

"Believe me, I do," she murmured, and stood on tiptoes, arching into him. "And I may lack experience in this area, but I read a lot. I know precisely what I want."

And she whispered something into his ear that seared every cell in his body.

He groaned. "Aw, Gabby. This is a mistake. You're not the kind of girl for cheap sex."

"Cheap sex isn't what I want from you, Joe Carpenter. I could have had cheap sex any time I wanted over these years. I'm not inexperienced because I haven't had the chance to lose—" she hesitated, nibbled at the base of his collarbone for a moment contemplatively before continuing "—my inexperience. I've had plenty of opportunities if cheap sex was all I wanted."

Joe cupped her shoulders, keeping her at a distance that didn't singe his nerves with flash fires. "So, what is it you're after here?" He cleared his throat. "If you don't mind telling me?"

"I'm after your heart and soul, tough guy, that's what. I'm offering you me, in marriage." Her gaze flicked away from his then, revealing her nervousness. "I'm offering to make an honest man of you, Carpenter.'' She tugged at his shirt, trying to pull him closer.

She'd managed to stun him immobile. "Marriage?"

"Yeah," she said with satisfaction. "You. Me. Oliver. Marriage. Family. I think it's a great idea. And so I'm proposing to you. Of course," she added earnestly, "I'm also trying to seduce you, but that's a separate issue."

He couldn't think. "Gabrielle, this is craziness. You deserve someone like, what's his name? Padgett?" He raked his hands through his hair. "Right. Someone like that."

"Nope." She trailed a finger along his mouth, distracting him. "I deserve you. And you deserve me, too, Joe, if you'd think about it."

"Damned if I can think of much of anything right now, sweet pea," he said, managing to laugh. "You're making me crazy, you know."

"Am I? Really?"

He heard the trepidation in her voice and was moved by it. "Yeah," he admitted. "You are."

"Oh, good. I'm trying to, you know."

"I figured that out." Deciding that the best defense was a well-maneuvered offense, he enclosed her in his arms and swept her up, carrying her back to the couch—no, not the couch, he decided with the last remaining bit of conscience still alert in his overheated brain—the straight-back chair. Once there, he held her still in his arms. "Look, Gabrielle, you're not thinking clearly. This isn't what you want." He waved toward the room, himself.

Her face turned serious, its sweetness weakening him in spite of everything. "Joe, I mean exactly what I'm saying. Oliver needs a woman in his life as well as a father. He needs the kind of stability I could offer him. As for you, I think I've loved—"

He covered her mouth. "Don't say it, Gabby. You can't take back words once said."

Holding his gaze with hers, she pushed his hand away. "I

think I've loved you since I was fifteen and you kissed me. My first kiss. I never wanted anyone else but you, Joe. And I want you now. With every fiber of my being, I want you. This isn't a sudden impulse on my part. It's been a gradual dawning of the light, you might say. It took me a while to sort out my motives and feelings, but I want you and Oliver in my life. For good. I want us to be a family and to celebrate Christmas and all the other holidays.'' She placed her hands on his cheeks, and her hands were warm. Not thinking, he pressed his mouth to her palm. ''This is the best offer you'll ever have in your life, Carpenter, and you'd be a fool to pass it up.''

It was an offer he didn't deserve, shouldn't listen to. He knew it was wrong, knew it wasn't fair to her, and he desperately sought the words to make her see how wrong for her marriage to him would be. ''You deserve better,'' he repeated.

''I know what I deserve, Joe. And I know it won't be easy. Oliver is mixed up about his feelings toward me, and this may be difficult for him. I don't know how hard it will be. But I'm a tough cookie, Joe.'' She smoothed her thumb across his mouth, and he couldn't help following that light touch, couldn't help taking a taste of her skin. ''I'm stubborn enough to wear him down. And, Joe,'' she murmured into the crook of his neck, ''I'm stubborn enough to wear you down, too. So surrender, cry uncle, and say you'll marry me. Christmas Eve.''

He discovered he didn't have the words to convince her how bad an idea marriage to him was for her. She would be taking on more than she could imagine. In one, final, desperate attempt to convince her, he told her about his doubts concerning Oliver's parentage. He was sure that knowledge would dissuade her.

It didn't.

She paused, thinking. ''That's a tough one, Joe. What are you going to do? Does he need to know? Does it make a difference to you? Because it sure doesn't make an ant hill's bit of difference to me. He's your son. It's your call, whatever you decide. Sure, I think he should know someday. Maybe not right now when he's had so many changes. But someday. And whatever you decide, I'd like to be there *with* you, by your side. Because I'm crazy about the little stinker. And one day, whether he knows it or not, he's going to be crazy about me.''

That easily it was done.

His conscience lay in shreds, demolished by the feel of her in his arms, defeated by the shining dream she held up to him, the dream that she kept telling him could be real.

He'd thought it would be impossible to schedule a church wedding. It wasn't. Gabby knew of a small church on the island. Quaint, rarely used, it was on the gulf side, its tall, old-fashioned windows opened to the tang of salt air.

It offered a midnight service and a Christmas morning prayer service. During the early part of the evening, the church would be empty. If they wanted, they could be married at eight o'clock Christmas Eve.

Gabby wanted. And Joe discovered that he wanted to give her what she so foolishly had decided was necessary to her.

On Christmas Eve, as he waited at the head of the church, Oliver beside him in a navy suit and white shirt, his small hand gripping Joe's, Joe felt the stirrings of his conscience. He looked down at Oliver and straightened the Christmas-theme tie Gabby had given him. ''You okay with this, squirt?''

''Maybe,'' Oliver said. ''Maybe not.'' He fingers tightened on Joe's. ''Milo will be my grandfather?''

Joe nodded.

''That's okay.'' Oliver scuffed the floor. ''And Cletis can visit?''

Joe nodded again.

''And all Gabby's going to do is live at our house for a while?''

''For good, son. Forever.'' And with that word, Joe finally understood that Gabrielle was the person he needed to fill the emptiness inside him. It was as if there were a spot inside his heart that had waited for her through all the ugliness and sadness and anger. She completed him.

The immensity of that knowledge filled him, pushed away the shadows and hate still lingering. Music swelled around him, and for a moment, he thought the music was playing only in his head.

But the whispers behind him told him otherwise, and he turned to face Gabrielle, the woman who'd proposed to him, the woman who'd insisted that, no matter how bad he'd been, she believed he was good enough for her.

A slim column of white moved toward him. Her hair lay loose and free on her shoulders, and the narrow fabric of her dress, some sliplike, silvery white thing, moved and shimmered in the candlelit shadows of the church. Every pew had been draped with evergreens and red bows. Thick white candles in heavy gold candelabra were at the aisle end of each pew, and tiny white flowers like stars made a waterfall down the sides.

Gabrielle carried a spray of glossy green leaves and more star-shaped flowers that draped down the front of her long dress. Floating from a wreath of flowers and gold stars, her veil covered her face, but he saw her eyes grow damp as Milo took her hand and gave it to him.

"I love you, Pa," she whispered to Milo before he took his seat beside Nettie in the front pew.

Gabby had told him earlier that Nettie wanted to do the flowers, and watching Milo take Nettie's hand in his, Joe wondered if Gabby might soon return the favor.

The fragrance of the flowers and candles and pine were an incense of the spirit, and Joe breathed in the sweetness as Gabrielle came to his side. Taking her hand in his, keeping Oliver's stubby hand clasped in his other, Joe faced her and took her, for better, for worse, in sickness and in health, to be his wife.

And he pledged himself to her, a promise that he would

give her the best of himself in every way, that he would care for her, too, in sickness and in health. That he would never betray her or harm her.

Oliver gave him the ring, and Joe slipped it onto her finger as her hand curled into his. Each moment seemed more and more unreal, a moment out of time where he was caught in a dream from which he didn't want to wake.

Lifting her veil, he stared at her. "Are you sure, sweet pea, really sure?"

"Of course I am."

Spoken with sweet certainty, her words pierced his soul, reverberated through him as he took her mouth with his.

All the guests, and there were more than Joe could have imagined, flocked back to Milo's. Milo, of course, had cooked. In her white dress, Gabby moved among their friends, Joe and Oliver at her side, until everyone, even Moon, had left.

Nettie and Milo had taken their wine into the kitchen, leaving Gabrielle, Oliver and Joe alone in the living room. The tree lights shone in the darkened room, and the three of them, suddenly quiet, sank onto the couch, Joe in the middle. Gabby leaned her head on his shoulder, and a faint, elusive fragrance rose to him from her skin, her hair.

On his other side, Oliver stirred. "Want your present, Gabby?"

She leaned forward, across Joe. Her breasts were a sweet, tempting weight against his thighs. "Sure, Oliver. I'd love to open a present."

"'Kay." Oliver raced toward the kitchen. "Come see! Presents!"

Gabrielle linked her fingers through Joe's. Everything she wanted was in this house. Everything she'd come home to find had been here, waiting for her. Pa. Nettie. Oliver.

Joe.

She'd wanted to make a perfect Christmas for her Pa. Instead, she'd stumbled on love. She'd taken a risk and tried to seduce Joe. *She'd* proposed to him. Because she loved him.

Oh, she knew her feelings toward him, and she knew, even in her inexperience, that she could arouse his passion. What his deeper feelings were, she could only hope and let her instincts guide her. If Joe came to love her, and she believed he would in time, believed in her most private heart that he would see how right their marriage was for all of them, well, then, she would truly have a miracle. She would have been given a Christmas gift that had no price.

Oliver handed her an awkwardly wrapped brown paper package. Glitter sprinkled onto her wedding dress as she opened the package carefully, spreading the decorated paper open. When she saw what lay on her lap, tears slid down her cheeks, tears that she couldn't stop, no matter how often she wiped them away.

"What's wrong, sweet pea?"

"You don't like it?" Oliver said softly, his voice cracking. "I wanted you to like it. I thought it would fix everything."

"Oh, sweetie, I *love* it. It's the most beautiful present anyone ever, ever gave me." She wanted to hug him close, but she didn't dare. She brushed his hair back from his face, and immediately it flopped back onto his forehead. "What a wonderful, clever idea." Then, with shaking hands, she held up the homemade star. The star was mounted on an aluminum-covered toilet paper roll. Glued to its front and back, shards of Irish crystal sparkled with rainbow reflections.

"I found the broken pieces in the drawer with Cletis's munchies. Is it okay?" Anxiety pinched Oliver's face.

"It's more than okay. It's, oh, Oliver, I can't believe that you thought of this." Tears slid down her face again, and Joe pulled her closer. She brushed Oliver's hair back once more, to let him know the wonder of his gift. "Joe, hold Oliver up to the tree. So he can put on the O'Shea star." Her hands still trembling, Gabrielle handed the star to Oliver.

Joe held Oliver up high, and, not saying a word, Oliver carefully settled the star at the top of the tree.

Milo snapped a picture of the three of them together by the

tree. Gabrielle held up the hem of her dress so that her snow-flake-flocked stockings would show in the picture.

"I might have known." Joe laughed. "My Christmas bride and her Christmas socks."

"*Stockings,* Joe," she said prissily. "Socks are cheaper. *These*—" she stuck one foot in his direction "—were very expensive."

"They look worth the cost." He encircled her ankle with his finger and thumb. "I'm developing quite a fondness for holiday socks."

She and Joe and Oliver curled up on the sofa, intending to watch the lights on the tree and the star while her dad drove Nettie home. Wanting Oliver to share every minute of Christmas Eve and to celebrate their marriage with them, she and Joe stayed at Milo's, waiting for him to return before they left for Joe's house and their wedding night. In the morning they would go back to Milo's for the rest of their Christmas celebration. Instead, tired and comfortable, drowsy with wine and emotion, they slumped together, Joe in the middle, and all three fell asleep.

Gabrielle woke to a splash of brilliant sunlight in her face. During the night someone had covered them with a blanket. She yawned, stretched and looked at Joe and Oliver. Both male Carpenters slept with their mouths slightly parted, Oliver making tiny snuffling noises.

She leaned over and kissed Joe. "Merry, merry Christmas, Joe. Want to stay here or go home and change? Christmas dinner will be much later. What would you like to do?"

As she climbed out from under the blanket, he stirred and turned to her. "What I'd like is my wedding night, sweet pea." He snaked his open palm up along her ribs, covered her breast. "I've been dreaming I got married. But I don't remember making love to my wife. And I'm hungry—for her, not for food."

She glanced quickly toward the sleeping child, blushed and said sternly, "Later. Tonight. If you're lucky."

"I plan on being very lucky," Joe said to her with a wicked, wicked gleam that woke up every ounce of her sleepy blood. "And so will you." He kissed her quickly, lightly. "Be." He kissed her again. "Lucky." He kissed her again, a long, lingering exploration that buckled her knees and left her wishing Christmas day were over.

With most of Gabrielle's clothes still at her father's house and in storage, she stayed at Milo's while Joe and Oliver left to shower and change before returning to the O'Shea household where everyone was coming for Christmas dinner.

With part of her mind on the turkey she was basting, Gabrielle tried to keep her thoughts away from the coming night. Her heart skittered and thumped every time she thought about herself and Joe, alone for the first time in the big bed he'd ordered for his—no, for *their* bedroom.

What if she disappointed Joe?

What if her inexperience bored him?

What if she couldn't—

"Darn!" She wiped gravy from the kitchen floor and washed her hands, letting the cold water run over her wrists and soothe her overheated self, even if it couldn't cool down her imagination. What would be, would be. She'd survive. Joe would, too.

Maybe, as Oliver was so fond of saying, she thought grimly and slapped the faucet off.

By the time Joe and Oliver returned to open the rest of the presents, she was a bundle of nerves and excitement and hope.

She'd changed into a green-and-burgundy-plaid taffeta dress that rustled satisfactorily when she walked, and as she answered the door she flushed as Joe's gaze moved slowly over her like the brush of his hands.

As Joe finally let his eyes leave her, he walked through the door, a lumpily wrapped package in his hands. Folding back the paper, he silently held out the object to her. Gold-painted macaroni covered a cardboard picture frame. Inside the frame, a chubby-faced three-year-old smiled back at her.

"Your idea, Mrs. Carpenter?"

Looking down, she touched the frame carefully, impossibly moved by the expression in Joe's eyes. "I helped. Oliver wanted to give you something special. I told him something he made would be part of himself, the best gift possible." She glanced at Joe. Made vulnerable by his love for his son, he was infinitely dear to her, and her heart almost cracked with the weight of her love for him. For his son. "You're a good man, Joe Carpenter. Your son loves you." Touching the frame again, she swallowed past the sudden lump in her throat.

"Thank you, Gabrielle." His hand slid to the back of her neck and he pulled her close for one fierce, tender, heart-dissolving kiss.

Oliver helped Cletis unwrap his presents, told Gabrielle about the bicycle Santa had left him at his own home and dug around under the tree, an expectant look on his face. He didn't say anything, though.

"Oliver, there's a special present for you, way to the back. It's that square package. See it?" Gabrielle held her breath as he pulled it out, dropped it and picked it up again.

"Mine?"

"Yours. From me." She waited, crossing mental fingers as he tore into the wrappings.

The star was Irish crystal. It hadn't been made by the same artisan that had made the O'Shea star. She'd had to drive to Tampa to have the star made in time for Christmas Day.

"You don't want the star I made you?"

"Oh, Oliver." She knelt and wrapped her arms around his tense body. "I love my star. It will always be on my tree. But this star? It's for you, for your children, for your trees in all the years to come. It's the *Carpenter* star. Yours, forever."

"Oh." He touched the edges carefully. "For me. Because you're marrying my daddy and going to live in my house." He laid the star carefully on the sofa. "Well, I don't want your old star," he sobbed, tiredness and frustration tearing through him as he wrapped his arms around Joe's leg. "He's *my* daddy. He wants *me,* not you."

"Of course he does," Gabrielle said. "I gave you your star because I love you. Because you deserve your own star. Because your daddy loves you more than anything in the whole, wide world. You're his son, and no one can take that away from you. No one can take your place. Not me, not anyone." She stooped next to him. "Do you understand how much your daddy loves you, Oliver? He would die for you. That's how much. A father's love can't be replaced. *Nobody* could ever take your place." Hugging him carefully, cautiously, she felt the tension seep from his small body. "Do you understand? Because it's important for you to know that, to know what a treasure you are. And *that's* why I gave you your crystal star."

"'Kay," he said, wrapping one chubby, sweaty arm around her neck. "Maybe I do."

He stayed with Joe for a while, and then Cletis galumphed by, Oliver took off after him, and Gabrielle wanted to waltz and sing carols and "eat Christmas cookies till I pop," she said, and nibbled on one of the cookies Oliver and she had decorated. "This is, without a doubt, my favorite Christmas of all."

And later, at Joe's house with Oliver sleeping down the hall, exactly as she'd dreamed, she unwrapped Joe's present to her. Joe had placed candles everywhere in the room, candles fragrant with the smells of Christmas. In the candlelight, the large, ungainly box sat at the edge of the bed. Pulling the sides of the box clear, Gabrielle gasped.

Inside the box was a narrow burled wooden chest with twelve thin drawers.

"Open the drawers, sweet pea." Lounging against the bedroom door, watching her alertly, Joe waited.

Each drawer was filled with neatly rolled-up socks. Thanksgiving, Halloween, Fourth of July, socks for each month of the year. And in each drawer, one pair of masculine socks, discreetly and seasonally patterned, lay next to the rest of the socks.

"Joe?"

"I thought I could get into this celebration thing. Maybe, maybe not," he said, echoing his son. "But I thought I'd give it a try."

She knew he was talking about more than socks. In the last drawer, a lumpy pair of Christmas socks wrapped a bulky object. Pulling the lump free of the candy-cane-patterned fabric, she gasped. In the darkness of the black material, light winked, something glittered.

"Oh, Joe," she whispered, holding up a crystal star. "Oh, Joe. You and Oliver, you both gave me Christmas back. My two stars."

He touched the star gently, ran his long finger over it, up her bare arm to her breast where her heart shuddered under her silk nightgown. He cupped his palm over her breast, and his expression was intent, focused on her, her face. "No, Gabby, you gave me Christmas. You gave me—"

Something she'd hoped to see stirred in his eyes, and she gathered her courage. "You love me, don't you?" Her throat closed.

"Yeah, sweet pea, I sure do. You're the gift I never expected in my life, wouldn't have known how to ask for. You're my very own Christmas miracle. Your goodness to me, to Oliver, to the people around you, leaves me speechless with awe. I don't deserve you, but I'll be double-damned if I won't go to bed every night for the rest of my life giving thanks for you." His voice turned dark and fierce. "I love you so much that it stuns me. It scares me, because if you walked away from me, I don't think I could survive."

"I'd never leave you, Joe. I've loved you all my life. I waited for you when I didn't even know I was looking for you." She tucked her finger in between two shirt buttons. And tugged. "Come to bed, Joe. Good girls can be bad, too, you know."

"Oh, I like the sound of that," he muttered into her ear as he lifted her into his arms. "Very promising idea. But did you know that bad boys can be very, very good? Given the right encouragement?"

He took the star off the bed and placed it on the nightstand, where it shimmered in the room, its light catching the flickering candle flames. Looking at it, he grinned. "Think we could have more than one Christmas tree?"

"Oh, Joe." With his shadowed face leaning over her, she couldn't think, couldn't breathe. "We'll have a houseful of trees and kids and celebrations."

She fumbled with the buttons of his shirt, love and passion making her clumsy. He helped her, guided her hands down the shirt to his belt. He helped her there, too, until they both lay skin to skin, his elbows supporting him as he moved in a rhythm she'd vaguely sensed long ago, that hunger as nothing compared to the need he created in her now with every touch and stroke. And, delighted, she began to see that she, too, was creating that same hunger in him.

This was what she'd waited for, this *togetherness,* this understanding that what he could make her feel, what she could make him feel, that what they were creating in this room where candles shimmered around them and their glow touched his face, hers, with light was a miracle of love and caring, a miracle worth waiting for.

Over his shoulder she saw a star blaze through the darkness of Christmas night, and as she took Joe to herself, his touch filled her with wonder. "Ah, Joe," she murmured into the curve of his neck as his hand curved over her and sent her into delicious shudders, "I'm *so* glad I'm not fifteen anymore."

"Me, too, sweetheart." His chuckle sent the loveliest shivers throughout her body. "Because I've waited too long already."

"So you have," she said primly, her skin prickling and tingling as he kissed his way up from her tummy. "And you

should be rewarded. I think I have just the reward for you.''
Lifting her arms, she wrapped them around his neck and pulled
his mouth to hers.

And by the light of the stars shining through the windows,
she proceeded to show him exactly, precisely what a good girl
could do when she loved the right man.

* * * * *

Beloved author *Judy Christenberry*
brings us an exciting new miniseries in

LUCKY CHARM SISTERS

Meet Kate in January 1999 in
MARRY ME, KATE (SR #1344)
He needed to avoid others meddling in his life. *She*
needed money to rebuild her father's dream. So William
Hardison and Kate O'Connor struck a bargain....

Join Maggie in February 1999 in
BABY IN HER ARMS (SR #1350)
Once Josh McKinney found his infant girl, he needed a
baby expert—quickly! But the more time Josh spent with
her, the more he wanted to make Maggie O'Connor his
real wife....

Don't miss Susan in March 1999 in
A RING FOR CINDERELLA (SR #1356)
The last thing Susan Greenwood expected was a marriage proposal! But cowboy Zack Lowery needed a
fiancée to fulfill his grandfather's dying wish....

A boss, a brain and a beauty. Three sisters marry for
convenience...but will they find love?

THE LUCKY CHARM SISTERS only from

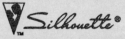

Silhouette®

Available wherever Silhouette books are sold.

Take 2 bestselling love stories FREE

Plus get a FREE surprise gift!

Special Limited-Time Offer

Mail to Silhouette Reader Service™

3010 Walden Avenue
P.O. Box 1867
Buffalo, N.Y. 14240-1867

YES! Please send me 2 free Silhouette Romance™ novels and my free surprise gift. Then send me 6 brand-new novels every month, which I will receive months before they appear in bookstores. Bill me at the low price of $2.90 each plus 25¢ delivery and applicable sales tax, if any.* That's the complete price, and a saving of over 10% off the cover prices—quite a bargain! I understand that accepting the books and gift places me under no obligation ever to buy any books. I can always return a shipment and cancel at any time. Even if I never buy another book from Silhouette, the 2 free books and the surprise gift are mine to keep forever.

215 SEN CH7S

Name	(PLEASE PRINT)	
Address	Apt. No.	
City	State	Zip

This offer is limited to one order per household and not valid to present Silhouette Romance™ subscribers. *Terms and prices are subject to change without notice. Sales tax applicable in N.Y.

USROM-98   ©1990 Harlequin Enterprises Limited

THESE BACHELOR DADS NEED A LITTLE TENDERNESS — AND A WHOLE LOT OF LOVING!

January 1999 — A Rugged Ranchin' Dad
by Kia Cochrane (SR# 1343)
Tragedy had wedged Stone Tyler's family apart. Now this rugged rancher would do everything in his power to be the perfect daddy — and recapture his wife's heart — before time ran out....

April 1999 — Prince Charming's Return
by Myrna Mackenzie (SR# 1361)
Gray Alexander was back in town — and had just met the son he had never known he had. Now he wanted to make Cassie Pratt pay for her deception eleven years ago...even if the price was marriage!

And in **June 1999** don't miss Donna Clayton's touching story of Dylan Minster, a man who has been raising his daughter all alone....

Fall in love with our FABULOUS FATHERS!

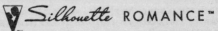

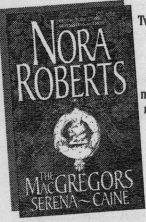
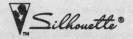

Silhouette ROMANCE™

COMING NEXT MONTH

#1342 THE BOSS AND THE BEAUTY —Donna Clayton
Loving the Boss

Cindy Cooper dreamed of marrying her boss, even though she doubted handsome executive Kyle Prentice would look twice at a plain Jane like her. But when Cindy's true beauty was revealed, could she trust that Kyle's sudden attraction was more than skin-deep?

#1343 A RUGGED RANCHIN' DAD—Kia Cochrane
Fabulous Fathers

Stone Tyler loved his wife and his son, but tragedy had divided his family. Now this rugged rancher would do everything in his power to be the perfect daddy—and recapture his wife's heart—before time ran out....

#1344 MARRY ME, KATE—Judy Christenberry
The Lucky Charm Sisters

He needed to prevent his mother from pushing him up the aisle. She needed money to rebuild her father's dream. So William Hardison and Kate O'Connor struck a bargain. They'd marry for one year, and their problems would be solved. It was the perfect marriage—until a little thing called love complicated the deal....

#1345 GRANTED: A FAMILY FOR BABY—Carol Grace
Best-Kept Wishes

All Suzy Fenton wanted was a daddy for her sweet son. But sexy sheriff Brady Wilson thought his able secretary was looking for Mr. Right in all the wrong places. And that maybe, just maybe, her future husband was right before her eyes....

#1346 THE MILLION-DOLLAR COWBOY—Martha Shields
Cowboys to the Rescue

She didn't like cowboys, but rodeo champion Travis Eden made Becca Lawson's pulse race. Maybe it was because they had grown up together or because Travis was unlike any cowboy she had ever met. Or maybe it was purely a matter of the heart....

#1347 FAMILY BY THE BUNCH—Amy Frazier
Family Matters

There was never any doubt that rancher Hank Whittaker wanted a family—he just wasn't expecting five children all at once! Or beautiful Nessa Little, who came with them. Could Nessa convince the lone cowboy to take this ready-made family into his heart?